BRODY BOONDOGGLE

The Rock of SARRAKA

A Spirit Animal Adventure

GARY KARTON

Illustrated by Samuel Valentino

BRATTLE
PUBLISHING GROUP

ISBN-10: 0990587258
ISBN-13: 978-0-9905872-5-5

Printed in the United States of America
First edition, January 2018

Book Design by Bumblecat Design and Illustration
Illustrations by Samuel Valentino

Dedication

To William, Oliver, Franklin, and Lucas.
And to Hiro, too.

Part I

The Breakout

chapter
1

Laga, Laga, Laga

Punching Crab sat alone in a dark cell in a Mexican prison. That's what happens when you feel so completely betrayed by a fish named Felonious that you jump on the first bus out of town and you keep heading south until you cross the border into Mexico. Then you start doing things that crabs your age shouldn't do, and before you know it, you're stuck in jail, and, instead of Punching Crab, everyone is calling you by your new prison name: El Pantsing Crab.

"Laga, laga, laga," Punching Crab repeated in the same way he did as a young crab when he would get so nervous or confused it seemed his brain and his mouth were no longer friends.

At first, hearing these words over and over made the prisoners believe Punching Crab had spent too much time in the steam room. But then his fellow prisoners got to know Punching Crab, and once they got to know him, it didn't take long until they started to like him for exactly who he was. They loved that he danced in the shower, that he believed he could identify colors by their smells, and that he carried around a golden acorn because he was convinced it was magic.

But what they loved most were his stories about an unusual 12-year-old boy named Brody Boondoggle, who had the powers of any animal he could imagine. Punching Crab told inspiring tales about how Brody teamed up with his big brother, Jake, and their hard-of-hearing Grammy to open the portal to the spirit-animal world known as Sarraka so he could save a magical creature called an Akaway.

But along the way, Brody was outsmarted by a diabolical video-game inventor named Uncle Skeeta, a spirit-animal guru named Felonious Fish, and Brody's ex–best friend Rudy, three names Punching Crab refused to ever say out loud again; so instead, he simply called them "the Scallywaggers," which is another way to say "bad guys."

The Scallywaggers had lied and connived and executed a perfect plan to enter the spirit-animal world and capture its powers. Now, Brody Boondoggle was desperate to find a way back into Sarraka so he could help the last Akaway and all the other spirit animals defend their home.

"But how will this Boondoggle character stop the Scallywaggers?" It was a common question from Punching Crab's fellow prisoners. "It seems the Scallywaggers are always one step ahead."

And secretly, Punching Crab worried about the same thing.

"I've given that a lot of thought, and the truth is, I have no idea," he answered, squeezing tightly on the golden acorn. "I just have to believe he has a magical plan."

Laga, laga, laga.

chapter 2

A Magical Plan

"¡Deténganse!" said a bearded prison guard in a spirited tone. And even though it was Grammy's and Jake's first time in Mexico, and they didn't speak the language, they were pretty sure the Spanish-speaking man was ordering them to "freeze."

It was not an unreasonable request. After all, it was the middle of the night, and Jake and Grammy were trying to break into one of the most heavily guarded prisons in all of Mexico. The prison was called La Casa Sin Salida, or "The House with No Exit," because once you were in this prison, you were probably never getting out.

There were security cameras almost everywhere. Two guards dressed in long-sleeved tan shirts with black cargo pants and combat boots were perched high in a tower on constant surveillance, meaning they were watching as Jake used the balance and agility of an ocelot to climb the 50-foot wall that protected three sides of the prison.

The guards in the tower alerted a dozen more guards on the ground that Jake was using those same spirit-animal skills to weave himself through circles of barbed wire, slide around the corner of the courtyard, and open the side gate so Grammy could sneak into the prison as well.

"¡Salgan con las manos árriba!" ordered the guard as his partner flashed a giant spotlight on Jake and Grammy, who could only squint back and shrug because they really had no idea what they were being told to do.

"Aren't you going to answer?" Jake whispered to Grammy.

"Oh, I think you're a lovely dancer," answered Grammy, circling her hips as if she were twirling a Hula-Hoop. "Really got that hip action working for you. But is that something you really want to talk about now?"

Jake rolled his eyes and took a half step closer to Grammy.

"I said, 'Aren't you going to answer?'" Jake whispered just a little louder.

"Oh," chuckled Grammy. "That does make more sense." She hesitated and added, "Did he ask a question?"

"I have no idea," said Jake. "I thought you were going to learn Spanish."

"Oh, my love, I'm learning right now," said Grammy. "And it's such a beautiful language."

Jake shook his head and took a deep breath.

"Okay, I've got this," he whispered, his mind racing as he tried to remember one of the few Spanish phrases he and Brody used when they played global cops and robbers with the neighborhood kids.

"Ahora mis zapatos son donas," Jake proclaimed. He smiled at Grammy with pride. Grammy smiled back with unconditional love, meaning she thought her oldest grandson was wonderful, even though what he actually said was, "Now my shoes are donuts."

The guard shook his head and mumbled to himself, "Ay caramba," before repeating his command in English.

"Step away from the gate with your hands up."

This time Jake and Grammy understood. But understanding and obeying are two different things, and Jake and Grammy did not travel all the way to Mexico to surrender so easily.

"We're looking for my grandson's dog, Tackle," Grammy tried to explain.

"This is a prison," the guard snapped loudly. "This is not the place for fun and games."

"Oh, every place is a place for fun and games," replied Grammy. "There's nothing more important." Grammy pointed behind the guard as if someone were actually there, and when he rotated his head, Grammy turned to Jake and whispered, "Let's go."

In a flash, Grammy was off. Now Grammy might have been a grandmother whose hearing was almost gone in her left ear and was starting to fade in the right, and who loved a generous portion of sponge candy before and after every meal, but she still had some moves, and she was using them all, cruising through the open courtyard like a chipmunk running from a weasel. Jake was running as fast as he could and was barely keeping up.

"Tackle, come here, boy!" Jake shouted repeatedly, as if he really believed his dog might come.

Tackle didn't come, but the guards did, which was just fine with Grammy and Jake, as they moved farther and farther away from the gate and into the underbelly of the prison. At first, it was just the one guard, but when he couldn't corral Grammy and Jake, another guard joined in, and then another. Pretty soon it was like a giant game of Monster Tag, as all the guards on the night shift had left their posts in an attempt to chase down the *loca abuela*, which Grammy was later proud to learn meant "the crazy grandma."

Of course, these were skilled and experienced guards, so it didn't take long until Grammy and Jake were completely surrounded.

"I must say, I do love your spirit," said the bearded guard, breathing just a little heavier than he would have liked to admit. "But there is nowhere left for you to run. The game is over. And now, you will have to answer to La Tarántula."

As the guards moved in to secure the new prisoners, they heard a faint sound coming from the other side of the courtyard. A few seconds later, the sound was louder.

"Arf. Arf."

All the guards turned to see a puppy happily bouncing toward Jake as if he didn't have a care in the world.

"Tackle!" yelled Jake.

The guards continued to focus on the beagle-shepherd mix as he pranced and danced and ran right up to Jake and jumped into his arms. Which, of course, meant the guards weren't looking at the only other way to enter the grounds of the prison—the one that required a half-mile swim through the powerful waves of the Pacific Ocean, an almost impossible challenge at any time, let alone in the middle of the night. Unless, of course, you had the power of the Akaway.

The Power
of the Akaway

Brody Boondoggle was wearing a full-length black wetsuit that made him appear more like a harbor seal than a 12-year-old boy, which made perfect sense, because that was the animal Brody thought about as he swam through the raging waters of the Pacific Ocean. And just thinking about the harbor seal's skill and grace in the water gave Brody those abilities, too. That's the power of the Akaway—and it was growing stronger in Brody all the time.

Brody dashed out of the water and peeled off his wetsuit, leaving him in his favorite pair of blue jeans and a gray T-shirt that read, "Welcome to the Brodeo."

He snuck down the isolated beach outside the prison, paused behind a giant hackberry tree, and placed his hand just above his left eye. That's where his scar used to be, the one he got when he followed his instincts to pet a magical creature that nobody had ever seen before—the one that connected him to the Akaway during his first adventure. But that adventure was over, and so that scar was long gone.

Now, Brody possessed a different connection. He slid his hand down just slightly, completely covering his left eye so he could see only out of his right—the same right eye that had recently turned from a hazel green to a cotton candy pink, just like the eyes of the Akaway.

At first the change felt odd—pinkeye is usually something kids want to avoid. But after a short conversation with Grammy, Brody understood that two different-colored eyes made perfect sense—one eye to stay focused on his world and his current mission, and the other eye to focus on Sarraka, to see what the Akaway sees.

Brody took five deep breaths—in through his nose and out through his mouth—and just like that, he was calm and focused. He scurried up the hackberry tree and surveyed his surroundings, trying to gather as much information as possible: where the rest of the guards were lurking, exactly how the other trees blocked the light coming from the full moon, the best way to return to the beach once the mission was accomplished.

Just as Brody was about to head in one direction, a strange feeling hugged him like a mama koala hugs her joey. Brody closed his left eye and focused in the air with his eye that was the perfect shade of pink. That's when he saw a bird circling high above him. At first, Brody was worried that the bird would draw the attention of the guards, but they didn't have the eye of the Akaway. Only Brody could see the bird slowly descend, gliding down from the sky softly and smoothly until it finally landed on Brody's outstretched arm.

Brody offered a welcoming smile as he studied its small head and neck, long and wedge-shaped tail, and broad, pointed wing. It had strong muscles in its chest, and Brody knew this bird had flown a long distance to get here.

"You're a passenger pigeon," Brody whispered, and the

bird responded with a "keck, keck," that let Brody know he was right.

"But that's impossible—you don't exist anymore," Brody said, and he was right again. The passenger pigeon had once been the most common bird in North America, but hunters and the destruction of its habitat took its toll on the passenger pigeon, and the species became extinct more than 100 years ago.

"So, how are you here?" Brody asked.

Of course, the passenger pigeon couldn't answer, at least not in English (or even Spanish), but he let out a subtle "keck, keck," that reminded Brody that even though many of the guards were distracted, there were plenty more lurking nearby, and he needed to act fast. The bird turned his head toward a tall tower on the opposite end of the prison. The tower was swallowed by thick ivy that covered every inch of the walls like a blanket of darkness.

"Keck, keck," the bird repeated, and Brody could swear the bird was telling him, "That's the way you want to go."

"I was planning to go the other way," Brody explained softly, but the bird just answered "keck," which clearly meant, "Trust me."

Brody sighed and thought and stared at the tower. "I do trust you," he decided, and when he turned back to the bird, it was gone. Brody looked up, over, and all around, and finally saw the passenger pigeon flying away as if its time was up and it needed to get back to wherever it came from. Brody waved to the sky and whispered, "Thank you."

Once again, Brody took five deep breaths. In that time, his heartbeat slowed, his senses heightened, and his path was clear, which was a good thing, because when Brody looked again with his right eye, he could see that the path for the Scallywaggers was clear as well.

chapter
4

The Path for the Scallywaggers

It's not easy to describe a magical world that no one has ever seen before. It seemed kind of like the wide open wilderness where animals are free to roam and thrive as nature intended, but not really. Sort of like the perfect lake house, where there are infinite opportunities to run, swim, and have as much fun as you can imagine, but not so much. It was almost like your neighborhood playground on a perfect summer night, where all the kids are outside playing their favorite games until it is too dark to keep playing, and then they still play some more, but kind of not. Basically, it seemed exactly like all of your favorite places in the world, but nothing like them at all.

"This is Sarraka," declared Felonious Fish, and even though Uncle Skeeta and Rudy had never imagined such a place before they jumped through the portal on Brody's birthday, there was no doubt in their minds that they were finally standing in this magical world.

Felonious reached into the light-blue finny pack that he wore around his waist and pulled out a small, thick notebook titled *The Secrets of Sarraka*. He flipped through the pages so Rudy and Uncle Skeeta could see all the maps, diagrams, and guides.

"This notebook contains everything anyone could ever want to know about the spirit-animal world," explained Felonious. "It will help us answer any question and solve any problem."

"Where did you get it?" asked Rudy, but Felonious didn't answer. He was too busy studying a map to determine exactly where they were and where they needed to go. A few moments later, Felonious picked up his head and scanned the landscape until he found a long, narrow trail that perfectly matched the one on the map.

"This way," Felonious pointed, returning the notebook to the finny pack. Then he led Rudy and Uncle Skeeta on a journey that was tough and fun and beautiful in all the right ways—climbing majestic hills, hiking twisting trails, and riding the raging rapids of Sarraka.

They talked very little except to say things like, "I've never seen so many tree forts," or "I already have ideas for three new video games," or "Do you think penguins would make good pizza delivery guys?"

But mostly, they were lost in their imaginations, dreaming about everything this new world had to offer. For Uncle Skeeta, his dreams were about finding the next level of inspiration and creativity. After all, there was nothing more valuable for a video-game maker who wanted to continue inventing games that kids could not resist. "Control the kids and you control the future"—that was Uncle Skeeta's motto, and as they walked down the white sand at the edge of a beautiful lake, he knew he was closer to achieving this dream than ever before.

When Rudy closed his eyes, his mind took him to a place of power, revenge, and defeating Brody Boondoggle, once and for all. There was no doubt, Rudy wanted what Brody had: the power of the Akaway, the power to be someone people would know and remember. As he got into the kayak at the end of the dock and started paddling, he could feel that his dream was only getting stronger.

As for Felonious, his dreams were about love, or at least that's what he told himself. A long time ago, he was one of the leaders in Sarraka and a huge believer in its special connection to kids. But then the kids started to take more and more energy from Sarraka, and the spirit-animal world started to suffer. Felonious trusted that the kids would make it right, that they would reverse the trend and repay the debt they owed to Sarraka. He had believed in them, fought for them, and in the end they let him down. Felonious turned dark inside. He challenged the Akaway for control, tried to persuade her to give up on kids and focus solely on keeping Sarraka safe. He had lost that battle, and Felonious had left Sarraka in disgrace, but not before he stole *The Secrets of Sarraka* and swore to find a way back to the land he loved. This was his chance to defeat the Akaway, take over Sarraka, and protect it the way he knew was right: by making sure kids and their spirit animals would never be connected again.

La Tarántula

La Tarántula closed the door to the prison cell slowly but firmly, leaving Grammy, Jake, and Tackle alone with the woman who was considered so scary that she was compared to a large, hairy spider with fangs.

Her real name was Isabela, and she was the country's most feared warden, meaning that when it came to La Casa Sin Salida, she was in charge of everything. The rumor was that La Tarántula's heart was as cold as dry ice. But those who knew her best disagreed—you'd actually have to have a heart to be cold-hearted.

La Tarántula had long, light brown hair, much like a female tarantula. She wore a tan short-sleeved T-shirt, cargo pants, and black boots. Jake noticed a tightly wound rope attached to her hip. He imagined the rope easily could have passed for a spider's web, and he held Tackle just a little closer so he wouldn't get caught.

La Tarántula took a sip from a coffee mug that read, "Yo no discrimino. Odio a todo el mundo por igual," which meant, "I'm not prejudiced. I hate everyone." She motioned for Grammy and Jake to sit on the metal cot in the prison cell that was no bigger than a minivan. La Tarántula chose to stand so she could look down on her prey. She was calm, confident, and in control.

"¿Hablas español?" La Tarántula asked in a cool, soft voice.

"Oh, I would love an egg roll," said Grammy, licking her lips. "It's been a long day, and I must admit I am quite hungry."

La Tarántula glared at Grammy with fury and impatience. "I said, Do you speak Spanish?'" she repeated, raising her voice so Grammy was sure to hear.

"Oh, that does make more sense," chuckled Grammy. "Not yet, but I'm planning to learn. It's such a beautiful language, and I already feel its energy seeping into my spirit."

La Tarántula shook her head in disgust. "It's the middle of the night," she snapped. She threw the coffee mug against the bars, and it shattered into a dozen pieces. Two guards rushed to clean it up, and even Jake helped a little.

"At the very least, you are trespassing on my property," La Tarántula continued. "But I sense there is something else going on here. I could easily have you arrested."

As always, Grammy was calm. "I suppose you could if you wanted," answered Grammy, looking up at La Tarántula with her soft hazel eyes. La Tarántula waited for Grammy to finish, expecting some type of excuse or desperate plea for freedom similar to that of so many others who had been in Grammy's position. But Grammy just shrugged silently.

La Tarántula looked at Grammy as if she were a creature from a different habitat, an alien who didn't truly understand where she was or who she was dealing with. Confused about how to respond, La Tarántula rolled her eyes and switched her attention to Jake.

"What are you doing in my prison?" she asked. Her tone was sinister and cold.

Jake looked at Grammy, wondering how he should answer. Grammy just shrugged as if to say, "How about the truth?"

The problem was Jake didn't really know the truth, or, more specifically, whose truth to tell. After all, the truth was often different, depending on your perspective. For Brody and Grammy, the truth was that this was another journey into their imaginations, the next chapter of an unpredictable adventure in which they truly believed anything was possible. For Jake, the truth was different. "Different but good," as Grammy would say, but different nonetheless.

Jake would have loved to accept a universe filled with magical worlds and special powers and endless possibilities, but deep down, he was just too logical to truly believe. So instead, he was happy to let Grammy and Brody have their magical moments together, except for a few special occasions like this one when Grammy would ask Jake as a personal favor to come along.

"We're in the middle of a kind of important adventure," said Jake, and he tried to mean it. "And it has led us to your prison."

"And this adventure is worth risking your freedom?" La Tarántula asked Jake.

Jake considered the question. "Some people think so," he said, motioning his head subtly toward Grammy.

"And what about you?" asked La Tarántula.

Again, Jake paused thoughtfully. "I don't see everything in the same way as the Grammcracker here," he finally answered.

Grammy perked up when she heard her nickname. "El Jakester set up one of those Instagrammy accounts for me called @theGrammcracker," Grammy said proudly. "I have three followers."

La Tarántula shook her head back and forth. "You let your grandchild come to Mexico and break into a prison?" She didn't wait for an answer. "Do you understand what kind of things can happen to kids in these situations?"

"Wonderful things," Grammy smiled.

"Dangerous things," shot back La Tarántula. "Your precious little boy could get hurt, wounded, battered, bruised, bitten, damaged, dented, smashed, scratched, broken, trampled, or just emotionally scarred forever. What kind of grandmother are you?"

Grammy paused, trying to figure out if the question was rhetorical, meaning La Tarántula might not have been looking for an answer. But while Grammy considered whether or not to respond, a light on the guard's phone started to blink.

He handed the phone to La Tarántula, who spoke so quickly that neither Grammy nor Jake could understand. But they didn't need to. "There is another intruder on the loose," she told them. "A young boy, according to our surveillance camera."

La Tarántula glared at Jake. "Is this boy with you?" she demanded. "And don't even think about lying."

Jake didn't lie, but he didn't answer either. After all, he was an ocelot, not a rat (which is just an expression, of course, since rats are known to be smart and loyal and probably don't deserve such nasty reputations).

But Jake's silence said enough for La Tarántula, who had a gift for finding the truth from people who were trying to hide it. "He is with you," she said. "I can see it in your eyes." She shifted her gaze to the surveillance photos on the phone. "He's your brother."

She's good, thought Jake. But again, he said nothing. La

Tarántula might have figured out the truth, but Jake didn't feel the need to confirm it until the time was right, which only made La Tarántula angrier.

"We will find this intruder and capture him," La Tarántula promised. It was a promise she had made and kept many times, so she was just a little surprised to see a strange confidence show up in Jake's spirit.

"You don't seem concerned," La Tarántula noticed. "Tell me, what kind of big brother are you?"

The question took Jake by surprise. What kind of big brother was he? It was something he had never considered, and when Jake thought about it for a moment, he realized it probably wasn't up to him to decide.

"I guess you would have to ask my little brother," Jake replied, looking La Tarántula in the eye in the kind of way that earns respect, especially from your foes. "If you can catch him, that is," Jake challenged. "It might be harder than you think. My brother is annoying and cocky, but he has talents that I don't think you would understand."

Jake's tone cut deep into La Tarántula's spirit, and he could almost see her blood start to boil with rage. "It is you who does not understand!" snapped La Tarántula.

She walked away and slammed the cell door behind her, causing a loud, echoing "crash" that rang though the halls. A second later, she stormed back, stuck her head right up to the bars and whispered, "And nobody is that talented."

That Talented

Brody Boondoggle concentrated on a small insect about the size of a quarter called a leafhopper, because a leafhopper can accelerate 200 times quicker than the fastest bird. And that's exactly what he did.

He seemed practically invisible as he quickly maneuvered in and out of the shadows of the night, heading toward the tower on the opposite end of the prison—thanks to a passenger pigeon that no longer existed.

I must be losing my mind, Brody thought to himself, but then he shrugged, because deep down, trusting animals felt perfectly right. He remembered the golden toad, an extinct animal that mysteriously appeared several days earlier while Jake and Brody were battling over who ate more of the macaroni and cheese, or maybe it was over who was in charge of the remote control, or perhaps it was over who had a better memory—it's hard to remember, since they seemed to battle about everything. In this case, Jake couldn't see the colorful toad, but Brody was certain that the "croaks" meant that they needed to travel to Mexico to find a friend, who just might hold the secret to getting back to Sarraka.

Brody concentrated again before starting to climb the ivy vines as easily as if he were a spider monkey. He stopped briefly on the second-floor balcony. The window was locked, so he grabbed the vines and continued to climb.

He followed the same routine—climbing higher, checking windows, moving on—until he reached an empty balcony outside a small window near the top of the tower. It was open just a little, and Brody sensed that this window felt right. He glanced down and watched as a bunch of guards scurried around, trying to find the intruder who had tripped the silent alarm and then disappeared into the night.

Brody slowly and quietly lifted the window. He peered inside and then froze when he saw a girl about his age with round glasses and long, dark hair. She was perfectly calm, sitting at the kind of small desk you would find in an elementary school. Brody noticed that the girl didn't seem happy, and she didn't seem sad. She seemed to feel nothing at all, which is often the worst way to feel.

Brody cautiously placed one leg through the window as if it were completely normal for a total stranger to be sneaking around a Mexican prison in the middle of the night. When the girl did not protest or freak out even a little, Brody tried to slide the rest of his body through the window but caught his foot on the ledge and fell flat on his face. The girl smiled, if only slightly, which was worth the embarrassment.

Brody jumped to his feet and brushed the dirt off his pants and shirt. He offered a subtle wave that meant "hello," and the girl responded with an equally subtle wave, meaning "Hola."

There was a short silence while Brody rotated his head like an owl to quickly scan the room. It was dark, lit only by a few candles and the light from the moon. Brody noticed a wide brown dresser, a wooden desk, a tall bookshelf with books stacked to the ceiling, and a small, narrow bed tucked away in the corner.

It was obvious to Brody that this was not a prison cell, even if it was in the tower of a prison. It was just a bedroom, not much different from his room at Grammy's. Only instead of an aura of energy, this room contained an aura of emptiness.

Then Brody noticed something else—something vibrant and exciting. On the wall opposite the window was an enormous painting. Brody looked closer and saw mountains and stars and a large gully with a long, narrow bridge high above. The details were so profound, thoughtful, and deep that Brody could swear he understood the story the painting was trying to tell. It was about freedom and adventure and danger—all the things he loved, too. At the top of the painting were the letters *AIP*, and in the bottom right-hand corner were the names *Rosalina* and *Myles*.

"I'm Brody Boondoggle," Brody said, pointing to his chest. A second later, he pointed to the girl. "You must be Myles?"

The girl smiled a full smile this time, and Brody took just a brief moment to appreciate that it was a nice smile that maybe hadn't been used nearly enough. "Just kidding," he shrugged. "Are you Rosalina?" The girl nodded. Brody nodded back and was about to ask about Myles, but the sound of guards yelling below quickly carried him back to his mission.

"I'm looking for *mi amigo*," Brody said, proud of himself for knowing that *amigo* meant *friend* in Spanish. He spoke very slowly and very loudly, as if that might somehow break the language barrier, but that's not how language barriers are broken.

So when Rosalina stared back blankly, Brody described Punching Crab, using hand and body movements as much as his words, as if he were playing an international game of charades. There was a long silence in which Brody thought he could see Rosalina's mind slowly understanding.

"El Pantsing Crab?" she asked.

"What did you just say?" replied Brody anxiously. "Could you repeato?" He spun his index finger in a circle as if that were the official sign for *repeato*.

"El Pantsing Crab," Rosalina repeatoed, and just saying the name seemed to brighten her spirit. "¿El Pantsing Crab es tu amigo?"

Brody hesitated for just a moment to consider the name.

Pantsing Crab? he thought to himself. But he quickly decided it was close enough.

"Si, si," Brody said excitedly. "Do you know where I can find him?"

At that moment, Brody and Rosalina were interrupted by a firm knock on the door, followed by a loud whisper. Rosalina instructed Brody to remain silent by placing her index finger over her lips. Then she tiptoed to the door and silently turned the heavy lock, because she knew who was on the other side.

"Es mi abuela," said Rosalina, meaning it was her grandmother, who also happened to be in charge of everything that happened in the prison. "La Tarántula."

At first, Brody figured that was a good thing, and he wondered why Rosalina would lock the door. But when the loud whisper slowly changed to an impatient yell, Brody realized that maybe all grandmothers were not the same. Brody probably should have been shocked, or at least a little concerned, that the mission in this prison just became a little more complicated. But at that moment, he heard a loud whisper of his own deep down in his soul, and his focus immediately shifted from what he saw with his left eye to what he saw with his pink eye.

The Pleasant Tree

"Can you at least tell me where we're going?" asked Rudy, who had been paddling his kayak for what felt like way too long. His shoulders were aching, and his back was sore, but his mind felt strong with possibilities.

"To the Pleasant Tree," said Uncle Skeeta, who had been scanning *The Secrets of Sarraka.* He looked at Felonious, who nodded that Uncle Skeeta was correct.

"What's a Pleasant Tree?" asked Rudy.

"Just a nice thing you say to someone to get the conversation going," said Uncle Skeeta with a smile. "Like 'Nice weather we're having,' or 'How's your day going?' or 'Did you see that chicken on stilts?'"

Felonious tried to hide a smirk; after all, this was business, and business wasn't supposed to be fun. But Uncle Skeeta flashed that contagious smile, and Felonious couldn't help but smile back.

"Try to stay focused," Felonious lectured before turning his attention to Rudy. "To answer your question, the Pleasant Tree," he explained, taking a long pause between the words *pleasant* and *tree*, "is one of the oldest trees in the universe, and one of the most important. Its roots are spread all through Sarraka—through the hills and valleys and even the waters. This tree is one of a kind."

"Why do they call it the Pleasant Tree?" asked Rudy.

"Because its power comes from a perfect balance of harmony and peace and love. And it spreads that power throughout Sarraka."

"So we're going to chop it down?" suggested Rudy innocently. "And then we'll have the power?"

Felonious immediately ordered Rudy to stop paddling. He looked around cautiously to make sure nobody had heard Rudy's words. Then Felonious rose up on his tail so he could stare Rudy in the eyes as the kayak slowly rocked back and forth in the gentle waves.

"What type of monster would chop down a beautiful tree?" Felonious asked. He lowered his voice but kept the same serious tone. "You don't mess with nature in Sarraka —or anywhere else," he lectured. "Listen to me carefully, because this is important. I would rather see Sarraka destroyed forever than have its spirit slowly devastated by killing trees, polluting the air, and poisoning the waters. You don't do that to something you love."

"Hey, chillax," interrupted Uncle Skeeta. "No one wants to destroy Sarraka. Let's stay focused here. I think the kid just wants to know how we get what we came for."

Felonious took a deep breath to chillax. Then he spoke calmly but sternly. "We will commit no crime. We will hurt no creature. We will ravage no land," Felonious said. "That will just bring attention to ourselves, and we cannot control the spirit animals in Sarraka if they know we are here to take over the land. Besides, we couldn't chop down the Pleasant Tree if we wanted to. No, no, no. That tree is too powerful."

"Where does that power come from?" asked Rudy.

"Now that's the right question," said Felonious, nodding his head.

He motioned for Rudy and Uncle Skeeta to continue paddling as he explained that the Pleasant Tree did not grow from a seed, like every other tree. Instead, the Pleasant Tree sprouted from a rock—a very special rock known as the Rock of Sarraka. This rock came from deep under the ground, at the very core of Sarraka.

As the Pleasant Tree grew taller, and its branches, twigs, and leaves continued to blossom, it lifted the Rock of Sarraka from the center of the world, out of the ground, and higher and higher into the air where it stood as a symbol of hope.

"The Rock of Sarraka doesn't just represent Sarraka," emphasized Felonious. "It *is* Sarraka—its power, its spirit, its heart."

"So if we can control the Rock of Sarraka," said Uncle Skeeta, his eyes growing wide, "we will control the power. And all our dreams will come true."

"Now you got it," said Felonious. "I'll have control of Sarraka, and it will be preserved and protected the way it was meant to be, without any interference from slimy, sneaky, miserable kids." He looked at Uncle Skeeta. "And you'll have all the secrets you need to create new video games, control those kids, and have the best business the world has ever seen." Finally, he turned his head slightly to the right. "And Brody Boondoggle will no longer have the power of the Akaway." Felonious smiled and pointed at Rudy. "You will."

No Ordinary Kid

Brody took five deep breaths—in through his nose and out through his mouth—and just like that, his spirit-animal skills helped him refocus on what he could control instead of what he could not. Rosalina and her grandmother were clearly battling, and even though he didn't understand the words that Rosalina used to respond to La Tarántula, he could tell by the tone in her voice that Rosalina was protecting him, maybe saying something like, "There's nobody in here" or "Just leave me alone."

But it was just as obvious that La Tarántula knew better. She might have been cold-hearted, but she was also cool-headed, so she understood that when two strangers and a mutt stroll innocently into a prison in the middle of the night, there is probably something that's not so innocent going on.

Once again, the talking turned to yelling, which turned to pounding, and Brody predicted La Tarántula wouldn't stop until he was captured—or worse.

Brody understood that finding Punching Crab was his last hope to get into Sarraka. But at the same time, something didn't feel right. This was his fight, and he knew he couldn't risk hurting an innocent girl, especially when he had a feeling she had been hurt before.

Rosalina looked at Brody and nodded as if to say, "I'm sorry about this," and Brody looked back as if to say, "Don't be. I've already put you in enough trouble." He didn't know how he would escape, but that was his problem. Brody offered one more smile, turned, and made a dash for the window.

He was about to maneuver himself back out onto the balcony when he heard one of those words that means the same in both Spanish and English.

"No."

Brody turned around and heard it again.

"No," repeated Rosalina in a powerful tone that Brody figured had been hiding in her for too long, just waiting for the right time to escape. And that's when Brody noticed something else. With every bang against the door, there seemed to be a new spark growing inside Rosalina's soul, like a tiny fire taking in oxygen and growing stronger and stronger. Rosalina's mind was racing, evaluating the space, time, and options like a *chica* with a strong connection to her spirit animal.

This is why you sent me, Brody thought, as if the passenger pigeon could actually hear him. Brody heard a subtle "keck, keck," as he reached into his pocket and grabbed one of the special rocks that were now always there when he needed them.

Trust your instincts.

It was the voice—the one that guided Brody when he needed it most. The one that showed him when the time was right to connect other kids to their spirit animals, which was without a doubt the most important power of the Akaway.

Trust your instincts. And Brody listened. When he did, things instantly froze. Brody's body felt warm, but right. He took a deep breath, and a few seconds later, everything moved in super slow motion.

THUMP, thump, thump, thump.

The beat seemed to be coming from two places: in Brody's own chest and directly in front of him. The beats were synchronized. Rhythmical. Perfect.

When Brody looked up, Rosalina was gone. In her place stood a small dark-brown creature with short legs, a long tail, and a hard shell on its back.

"You're an armadillo," said Brody, and then immediately realized he needed to be more specific. "I want to introduce you to your spirit animal," he explained in a language that he and Rosalina now shared. "You're an armadillo."

The only thing Rosalina knew about an armadillo was that it was Spanish for "little armored one," which immediately seemed right, and that feeling made her spirit just a little bit brighter.

Rosalina looked around her neck. Hanging on a leather cord was a rock with the imprint of a hard shell and a tail. It represented the armor that protected the special creature that was thoughtful and smart, but preferred to be alone, sleeping during the day and working through the night.

Rosalina seemed to gain more and more strength and understanding by simply rubbing the rock between her index finger and thumb. Finally, she looked up, stared into Brody's eyes that were two different colors, and smiled. "You're no ordinary kid, are you?" she asked.

Brody Boondoggle looked back, shrugged, and simply replied, "There's no such thing."

chapter
9

Blubber

Brody Boondoggle rubbed his hands through his long, straight hair and watched as the armadillo in Rosalina took charge. Without hesitation, she dashed to the corner of the room, leaned her shoulder into the side of the dresser and twisted it away from the wall. At first, Brody thought Rosalina was planning to push the dresser in front of the door like a barricade to delay the guards from busting in, but instead, she calmly moved her fingers along the back of the dresser.

A sly smile appeared on Rosalina's face when her hands reached the perfect spots. She curled her fingers into a fist and pounded them twice at the same time.

Instantly, the back of the dresser popped open. Rosalina reached into the secret compartment and pulled out what seemed to be a combination of a dark green backpack and a hooded sweatshirt.

"What is it?" asked Brody, his eyes wide with anticipation, meaning he knew it was something important, and couldn't wait to hear all about it.

"This is the Hoodster," beamed Rosalina.

Rosalina explained that the Hoodster was a special backpack that would provide them with all the tools and tricks they would need for their mission, and, after a quick review of all the straps and pockets and zippers, Brody's only thought was that he wanted one just like it.

Rosalina slid her arms through the straps of the bag and flipped the hood over her head. It was as if that simple move magically transformed her into a new kind of hero, complete with costume, utility bag, and secret identity.

Brody also noticed that the same three letters—*AIP*—that were at the top of the painting on her wall also appeared on the top of the Hoodster. He had a feeling those letters were important and was about to ask what they meant when he heard a loud "BOOM."

Before Brody could think about what to do first, Rosalina was already in action.

"They're trying to break in," Rosalina predicted. "Push the dresser in front of the door." While Brody did, Rosalina darted to the opposite side of the room and started pulling the rug from under the bed, revealing a hidden panel in the floor about the size of a checkerboard.

As the banging from the guards grew louder and more consistent, Rosalina looked to Brody, who was concentrating on the massive blubber of an elephant seal as he leaned his weight against the door to keep it shut.

When Brody offered a playful wink, Rosalina quickly looked away, but she secretly smiled as she reached into a side compartment of the Hoodster and removed a long, flat instrument that fit perfectly into the grooves of the hidden panel. A few quick twists and the panel was open. Rosalina then unzipped another pocket and removed a thick rope.

"BOOM!"

The banging on the door was more intense, as if the guards had started using a battering ram, and Rosalina noticed the door wobbling on its hinges as the guards hit it again and again. Still, the pressure only made her calmer, and she moved with rhythm and purpose. It was as if this were a dance she had been practicing in secret for years and was simply waiting for the right music and inspiration to perform it for real.

Rosalina quickly tied the rope to the corner leg of the bed frame and darted back to the square hole in the floor.

"Follow me," she whispered, maneuvering her legs, waist, shoulders, and finally her head safely through a small opening in the floor. Brody immediately darted from the door, dropped to the ground, and slid his feet, then his legs, then his waist through the hole. But that's as far as he got.

"What are you waiting for?" asked Rosalina. "Why did you stop?"

"It wasn't on purpose," Brody promised, shaking his hips. But it was no use—the blubber from the elephant seal was great if you wanted to be protected from extreme cold, and it even helped if you were trying to make sure a door wasn't knocked in by guards in a Mexican prison, but it kind of got in the way when you were trying to escape through a small opening in the floor.

"Um, I don't mean to rush you," said Rosalina, "but if they catch you, you'll be spending more time with El Pantsing Crab than you'd like."

Why does she keep calling him El Pantsing Crab? thought Brody, before shaking his head and instructing his mind to focus.

"BOOM!"

"I'd say about two more booms," Rosalina predicted, pulling Brody's legs as he continued to wiggle, waggle, and squirm.

"BOOM!"

"Let me get back up there," said Rosalina when it became clear Brody would not fit through the hole. "I can delay them while you escape. If one of us is going to be captured, it should be me."

"I have a better idea," replied Brody. "How about no one gets captured?"

He calmed his mind and concentrated less on blubber, even though the word made him chuckle, and more on a bloodworm and its flat, cylinder-like body that can fit through the smallest crack in the cement. Then he twisted his shoulders, wiggled his hips, and slid right through the hole.

Rosalina quickly yanked the rope to pull the carpet and the bed back in place. She used the same long, flat instrument to cover the hole with the panel just as the second and final BOOM caused the door to come crashing down, smashing the dresser into splinters.

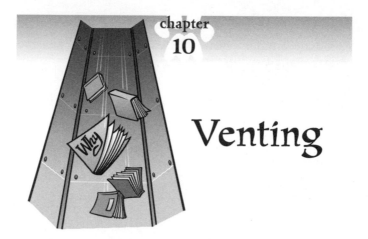

10

Venting

Rosalina sensed that Brody Boondoggle was just a little nervous, which made sense. He was currently in a long, dark, abandoned elevator shaft balancing on a tiny wooden ledge.

"All part of the plan," Rosalina whispered as the footsteps from the guards echoed above like rain falling on a metal roof. "Just do what I do."

Bracing her hands and knees against one side of the wall and her Hoodster against the other, Rosalina started lowering herself down the elevator shaft inch by inch.

"See?" said Rosalina, with a sly grin that was barely visible from behind the hood. "It's not that hard."

"Maybe not with that Hoodster to support you," commented Brody. "Where can I get one of those?"

"You can't," said Rosalina as she continued moving lower and lower. "There are only two of them in the world."

Where's the other one? wondered Brody for just a moment. Then he tried to think of an animal that could slide down a dark hole when one slip would mean a fall that could hurt even the toughest armadillo, but as he watched Rosalina work with such grace and ease, he decided just to copy her movements instead.

"Those *albóndigas* will never find us," boasted Brody, as he started to develop a rhythm of his own.

"Do you realize you just called them *meatballs?*" asked Rosalina.

"I just like saying *albóndigas*," admitted Brody. "The word makes me smile—kind of like *crotchety*, which is strange because *crotchety* means 'grumpy,' and if you're grumpy, you don't usually smile."

"Or *rapscallion?*" added Rosalina, describing a person who would actually smile, because a rapscallion loves mischief. But then Rosalina's tone changed to a more serious one. "Those *albóndigas* might not find us, but *mi abuela* will. It's just a matter of time."

And just as Brody was about to ask, "How can you be so sure?" he heard the legs on the bed screech against the floor, and the panel that protected their location start to shake.

Rosalina placed her index finger over her mouth and scurried down just a few more feet, where a steel grate covered an opening in the wall. She reached into her bag for another instrument that easily opened the grate.

"This way," she instructed, sliding into an air-conditioning vent. She removed the dark hood for a better look as Brody followed her into the vent, just as a small object came whizzing by his head. It ricocheted against the wall and landed at their feet.

Rosalina picked up the object. It was a paperback book that was in the shape of a triangle.

"This is probably only the beginning. Better settle in," Rosalina advised, as she casually flipped through a few pages of the book titled *Why?*

Brody studied the look on Rosalina's face. He was amazed that she was so calm. She didn't seem sad or even surprised that all the books from her room were whizzing by the vent one by one.

A dozen questions raced through Brody's mind. Who had the other Hoodster? Why was Rosalina's grandmother so angry? Who invented the washcloth and why? But before he could ask, the books stopped falling, and the moment was gone.

Rosalina replaced her hood, unzipped a pocket in the bottom of the Hoodster, and removed a small, thick map. As she unfolded the map, Rosalina explained that the prison was actually a castle owned by a notorious criminal, who the police could never catch because the castle had so many trapdoors and hidden paths. Eventually, the police decided that they would just lock the criminal inside and not let him out. "And that's how the castle became a prison," said Rosalina. "And I've mapped every inch of it."

She pointed to an area in the middle of the paper. "We're here in the vents," she explained. "Our best chance is to follow this air vent all the way to another shaft that will lead us down to the basement. Then it's a quick dash through this corridor, down these stairs over here and then . . . ," she pointed to the lowest point on the map. "We'll find *tu amigo* here."

"And we'll be safe from your grandmother and the guards?" asked Brody.

"Not a chance," said Rosalina, returning the map to the Hoodster. "My grandmother is stubborn and smart, and she won't give up until we're caught once and for all."

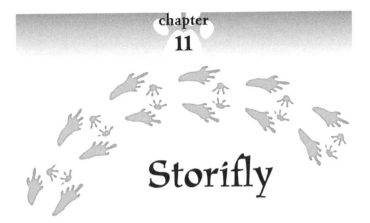

Storifly

The journey through the underbelly of the prison was cold and quiet, and sometimes treacherous. Brody had to work his hardest to keep up with Rosalina as they tackled what felt like a combination of a maze and an obstacle course, which was actually kind of fun if you didn't focus on the fact that you were running from a crotchety spider.

They talked very little except to say things like, "Grab on to those bungee cords," or "Climb down that ladder," or "Do you think trees should wear sunglasses?"

Then, after a long silence, Brody finally asked one of the many questions he couldn't hold in any longer: "Who is Myles?"

Rosalina froze in the middle of a tall ladder. Brody waited and added, "I saw his name on the painting in your room, remember?"

"I remember," replied Rosalina, cautiously continuing to climb down the ladder. "Why do you want to know?"

"I'm just interested, I guess," said Brody, thoughtfully.

Rosalina stopped again and glanced up at Brody, her mind racing, trying to decide how much to trust this unusual kid she had just met. Exploring the prison was one thing; exploring her most trusted secret was quite another.

Rosalina looked deep into Brody's eyes, first the one that was hazel green, then the one that was cotton candy pink. When Brody looked back, Rosalina couldn't help but see an obvious decency, meaning that even though Brody was clearly cocky and maybe even a little dark inside, he was also good and someone worth trusting.

"Myles es mi *hermano*," said Rosalina softly, and Brody was right to assume that *hermano* meant "brother." "He is also my best friend."

Is that possible? Brody thought to himself before asking, "Where is he? Does he still live with you?"

"Not exactly," said Rosalina. She took a deep breath and started moving faster down the ladder. When she reached a catwalk, she broke into a jog. "We don't have time for this."

"Sure we do," said Brody, following close behind. "My Grammy believes in this magic called *storifly*. If you tell the right story, it makes time fly."

Brody realized the idea sounded a little suspicious, so he decided it might help to start with a secret story of his own. He thought for a moment, and then told Rosalina the story about the last Akaway—about Grammy, about Jake, and the reason his eyes were two different colors. He admitted he felt terrible about being tricked by Uncle Skeeta, Felonious, and Rudy. He promised that he would never give up until he found a way into Sarraka. He even confessed that he was relying on the help of a few animals that were no longer alive.

"Wait a second, you see extinct animals?" asked Rosalina. "Do you know anyone else who sees them?"

Brody laughed. "No, it's pretty weird I guess. There's probably something seriously wrong with me." Rosalina shrugged and sighed as if she had more to say on the topic. Instead, she changed the subject. "Can I ask you another question?" she asked. Brody nodded. "What do you think it's like in Sarraka?"

Brody took a deep breath. He had considered this question many times, mostly in his visions and his dreams. "I think it's the place we go to when we let our minds wander and just be free," said Brody. "No distractions, no limits. Like a zip line directly into your imagination."

Rosalina nodded, and after a short pause, she agreed that there was magic in sharing. So as she ran and climbed and led the way through the prison, Rosalina shared her story about Myles.

Darting down another chute to the basement: "Myles and I grew up together right here in this prison. For most of my life, we spent almost all our time together."

Dashing through the corridor: "La Tarántula had very strict rules. I was barely allowed outside during the day and never at night. But hanging out with Myles somehow made everything better. He was sly and shy and loved to explore and play tricks on the guards. And they never caught him—not once. But he was restless, too, like he was meant to be somewhere else. His dream was to find a place no one had ever seen before."

Flying down the back stairs to the lowest point of the prison: "Myles had this feeling—a voice deep inside that was calling to him, telling him that it was time to go, and he couldn't ignore it any longer. He planned a way for us to escape, and we practiced all the time. But on the night we were going to leave, I got nervous. What if it didn't work? What if we got caught? I got so scared that I never tried. Myles understood, but he had a mission, like you. So he showed me how to build a secret compartment in the dresser, showed me how to create the Hoodster, as he called it, and told me that if I ever needed to find a way out, I would know what to do. Then he grabbed the only other Hoodster and left."

For a moment, Brody dreamed about what it would feel like to have a big brother like Myles. "I have a brother, too," said Brody. "I wish he would run away."

"Don't be so sure," Rosalina answered. "You might miss him when he's gone." Then she stood up just a little taller and spoke with a confidence that made Brody see why the passenger pigeon sent him this way. "After that night," she continued, "I told myself I would never let fear stop me from doing something again." She looked at Brody. "That's why I'm going to make sure you and your friend make it out of here."

Rosalina's *storifly* worked perfectly. By the time she added, "That's a promise," they had made one last sharp turn to the right and crawled through what appeared to be an empty fireplace. She used an ultraviolet flashlight from the Hoodster to locate a small mark on one of the walls.

"Remember I told you there were lots of trapdoors and hidden paths," Rosalina said with a proud grin. She softly pushed on the mark, and the wall on the other side of the fireplace slid open. "Well, here's one of them," she said. "It leads directly to the cell where tu amigo, El Pantsing Crab, is located."

"Why do you keep calling him that?" Brody was about to ask as he came around one more bend, but then his eyes widened when he entered a large open room with a small jail cell in the middle, and suddenly it didn't matter how Rosalina referred to his old friend. The only thing that mattered was that Brody was staring at him right now.

C_NNECT__NS

Grammy and Jake were mostly silent as they sat with Tackle on the metal cot. That's what happens when two people who "don't see things the same way" are locked in a cell together with nothing to do but wait. At first, Grammy asked Jake a few simple questions about what he liked best about the adventure and what he liked least, to which Jake gave simple answers like "breaking in" and "getting caught."

That led Grammy to say things like "everything happens for a reason," which just happened to be on Jake's list of top phrases that he didn't like or understand.

"What if everything doesn't happen for a reason?" Jake

asked. "What if things just happen, and then people try to invent the perfect reason after the fact? Don't you think that's possible?"

"Oh, anything is possible," said Grammy, which was also a phrase on Jake's list. *It's not possible for me to fly or break through this brick wall*, he thought, but instead of responding, he decided to simply stop talking, and since Grammy knew better than to force a conversation with a teenager, she simply thought about as many of the Spanish words as she could remember.

But eventually the silence only made Jake realize just how different he and Grammy still were. He knew that if it had been Brody stuck in a small, confined space with Grammy, they would have no problem talking and laughing and making time fly by imagining magical stories or inventing incredible new games. Jake and Grammy's favorite game seemed to be a silent contest.

Finally, Jake looked at Grammy and sighed. "Do you want to play tic-tac-toe?" he offered.

"Oh, I would never kick a black crow," said Grammy. "You should talk to someone about this anger toward crows. But I'm sure you'll work it out in time."

Jake opened his hand to reveal a piece of La Tarántula's coffee mug that he had kept when it shattered against the bars. He walked over to the bricks on the wall and scratched two straight vertical lines and two horizontal ones. He placed a big X in the bottom, right-hand corner.

"I said, 'tic-tac-toe,'" he repeated just a little louder. "Do you want to play?" And, of course, Grammy said, "Yes."

Tic-tac-toe turned into dots, which turned into hangman, as Jake continued to scratch away at the bricks on the wall. All the while, Jake was trying to find a way to ask the question he really wanted the answer to. Finally, he simply blurted it out. "Why do you make me do these things?" he asked loud enough for Grammy to hear.

"Oh, sweetie, I don't make you do anything," Grammy responded. "You're responsible for your own decisions."

"Maybe so, but you ask me for these favors, and it's pretty hard to say no," replied Jake. Grammy nodded as if to say, "Fair enough."

"I just don't see why I need to be here," Jake added. "All the magic and crazy adventures and things that make no sense. It might be fun for some people, but if you don't believe, then what's the point?"

"That's a beautiful question, my love," said Grammy. She stood up and gave her oldest grandson a huge hug. "I love the way you see things in your own way. The way you question what you don't understand. I hope you never change."

Then she grabbed the piece of coffee mug from his hand. "But if you're asking me the way I see things . . . ," she paused and started scratching small lines on the hangman board. While she did, Jake noticed a subtle sound coming from behind the wall after each scratch. It sounded like a soft echo, and Tackle agreed after a couple sniffs.

Jake shifted his focus away from the hollow wall and back to Grammy just as she finished scratching her eleventh line. "One of the most magical things I know really comes down to one simple word," Grammy continued, motioning for Jake to start guessing letters.

He studied the puzzle for a moment before guessing *E* and *R* and *T* and *S* and *N* and *A* and *L* and *P.* When he finally guessed the letter *C,* he had all the letters he needed to figured out the word that meant so much to Grammy: C _ N N E C T _ _ N S.

"Connections?" Jake guessed. "What's so important about connections?"

"Only everything," replied Grammy. "True connections just might be the greatest magic in the universe. Like the one you have with your brother. It's those connections, if we allow them to happen, that make everything in life worthwhile."

Jake was pretty sure that he didn't understand a word Grammy was trying to say. "Brody has a connection with a lot of things, but I'm pretty sure I'm not one of them," said Jake without showing emotion, even though he felt just a little sad admitting that truth. "And there's certainly nothing magical between us."

Grammy just chuckled. "You're brothers," she said. "There's nothing more magical."

chapter
13

The Bars That Wouldn't Budge

"Punch," Brody whispered as he sprinted toward the cell. Rosalina had just finished attaching a small mirror to each of the security cameras to reflect the view so that when the guards looked at the monitors, everything seemed perfectly normal.

Brody stuck both arms through the bars as if he could magnetically pull Punching Crab closer, but he couldn't think of an animal that had that kind of power, so instead, he sounded more like a parrot, repeating over and over, "Punch, Punch, Punch, Punch."

Punching Crab cautiously turned his head. When he saw Brody, his eyes widened, and for an instant, Brody could see a glimpse of that hopeful spirit deep inside Punching Crab's soul.

"We're getting you out of here," Brody promised, and Rosalina was already on her way to a black box that hung on the wall—the one that contained the key to the cell and to Punching Crab's freedom. But when Rosalina entered a four-digit code into the keypad on the box, the box didn't open.

"Are you sure you're using the right code?" asked Brody, peeking over Rosalina's shoulder as she tried again and again.

"I oughta be sure," Rosalina answered. "It's been the same code since the day I was born. It's my birthday."

Brody focused on the numbers as Rosalina typed: 1229. "Interesting," Brody whispered. "That's my birthday, too." And he allowed himself just a moment to wonder exactly what that coincidence could mean.

"Well, *mi abuela* must not like that day anymore, because she clearly changed the code," Rosalina said. "That means two things. First, she knows we are here, so the guards will be coming like cockroaches. And second," Rosalina paused and turned her head to face Brody, "nothing is going to open those bars."

Brody stuck out his chest with a cocky arrogance. "Challenge accepted."

He took five deep breaths and started shaking the bars with the might of an ox, an elephant, and a dung beetle, which can pull more than 1,100 times its own weight. But the bars wouldn't budge.

Brody's face turned red, and his eyes started to bulge as he grabbed hold of the two bars right in front of Punch and tried to pull them apart while concentrating on a tiger, an anaconda, and an eagle, which is the world's strongest bird. But the bars still wouldn't budge.

A blue whale, a saltwater crocodile, a lowland gorilla. Thinking of all the toughest animals on land, sea, and air made Brody stronger, but not strong enough to bend or break the solid steel that surrounded his friend.

Finally, he let out a deep breath. "She might be right about the bars," he whispered to Punch. "But don't worry, I'll think of something."

Punching Crab rolled the golden acorn in his claw a little faster, looking for hope, but after being stuck in prison for so long, Punch had started to convince himself that maybe hope wasn't possible.

"It's probably just as well," said Punching Crab sadly, which might have been the last thing Brody was expecting him to say. Punching Crab never gave up on anything, certainly not when it came to Sarraka.

"What are you talking about?" replied Brody. "It's not just as well. What's going on with you?"

Punching Crab thought for what seemed like a long time, but was probably only seconds. He wondered whether or not to share the feelings deep inside that he had tried to keep hidden, not just from his friends but from himself—feelings about something that seemed even more important than trying to get back to Sarraka, at least at the time.

Finally, he turned his head and let them out. "It's not like I'm ever going to be a spirit animal."

Brody rubbed his hand through his hair and let out a long, slow breath.

"Spirit animal?" Brody replied. "Is that what this is about?" Punch didn't answer, so Brody continued. "Where is this coming from?" he said softly. "You're going to be a spirit animal, but not if we don't get back to Sarraka. And we have to move now."

"It's not true," Punching Crab replied. "Felonious used to tell me the same thing: 'You're going to be a spirit animal one day,' and I believed him. I've been trying and hoping and believing for too long—but not anymore. Sitting in this prison I've had plenty of time to think, and I finally realized the truth. Felonious is full of baloney. He's not my friend. He never was, and that's how I know I'll never be a spirit animal." Brody was about to respond, but Punching Crab didn't let him. "I'm not a cheetah, or a tiger shark, or even a sucker-footed bat." Punching Crab continued as he sunk into his shell. "I'm just a crab."

"Crabs are awesome," replied Brody. "They're fun. They have wisdom. They even carry around their own protection. What's better than that?"

"You tell me," Punching Crab responded, still in his shell. "Name one person who would want a crab as a spirit animal?"

Brody paused for a moment or maybe more while he considered the perfect response. But the silence said it all, and finally Punching Crab simply dropped his head and said, "That's what I thought."

Where They Are

Brody Boondoggle moved closer to the cell and slid down against the bars. For just a minute, Brody said nothing, which might have been the perfect thing to say. After all, he was one of the few people who really understood Punching Crab's pain. How it felt when you wanted something so badly and couldn't get it—like getting to Sarraka, or being a spirit animal. Or even worse, when you thought someone was your best friend, and then you realized maybe he wasn't.

Felonious and Punching Crab had been best friends for forever, just like Brody and Rudy. To think that they could be so far from that now seemed impossible—or maybe improbable, since nothing's impossible, or at least that's what Punching Crab used to believe.

Brody had spent so much of his time and energy trying to figure out how to get back to Sarraka that he never really took the time to digest the fact that he didn't have a best friend anymore. He glanced over at Punching Crab and noticed that he seemed worn down, listless, a shell of his former self. *That's the way I feel sometimes*, he thought to himself, and for just a few minutes he allowed himself to embrace those feelings, sitting still next to Punching Crab, alone but together.

Finally, Rosalina motioned to Brody that the guards were sure to be coming soon. It was time to leave. Brody nodded, took one more deep breath, and looked at Punching Crab.

"You were meant for more than this," Brody said. "We came a long way to get you, and we can do this. But we can't do it without you." Brody paused and smiled. "Even Jake is here, and you know he doesn't care about anything but his hair."

"Yeah, well I didn't want to tell you, but Jake and Grammy were captured by La Tarántula," said Punching

Crab. "They're locked up. And the word going around the prison is they're not getting out until you're captured, too."

Brody lifted his head to the sky and let out a deep, surrendering breath. "Locked up?" he repeated. "That wasn't the plan." Brody shook his head. "They should be waiting for us in an escape boat right about now."

Brody's thoughts suddenly shifted to a darker place. "And if I know Jake, he's going to blame this on me somehow." Brody shook his head. "If only he believed a little more. Maybe those animals would have warned him instead of me."

Punching Crab's eyes widened just a little. "What did you just say?"

"He's going to kill me," repeated Brody. "Then he'll tell me to toughen up." Brody dropped his head. "We haven't been connecting lately."

"I mean about the animals," clarified Punch. "What about the animals?"

"I don't know. I started seeing animals lately, actually extinct animals," explained Brody. "They've been helping me." He told Punch about the golden toad, who led Brody to Mexico even though it had already croaked, and about the passenger pigeon, who directed him to Rosalina. "It felt a little strange at first," Brody said, "but we wouldn't be here without them."

"It's not a little strange," beamed Punching Crab, kissing the golden acorn. "It's extremely strange in an absolutely perfect way. It takes a very special power to see extinct animals. I don't know anyone else who can do it."

Punching Crab paced around the cell, thinking about all the possibilities.

"Is seeing extinct animals a good thing?" asked Rosalina.

Punch rushed to the front of the cell. "To me, it's a very good thing," he answered. "It means there is still hope."

Punch took a second to figure out the best way to explain. "Those animals . . . those beautiful, caring, extinct creatures are Sarraka's final defense mechanism. And they want to help."

It was obvious that Brody and Rosalina still didn't fully understand, so Punch sat down and quickly explained the legend of extinction, which goes like this: When an entire species of animal is gone forever—like the dinosaurs or the dodo birds—they live in Sarraka, where they are free to roam and play as they were meant to do, safe from the pollution or poachers or whatever else led to their demise. But there has always been an unrest with many of these extinct animals, a calling deep inside that they were taken too early and never truly got a chance to make a difference.

"Don't you see? This is their one chance," said Punch, jumping to his claws. "This is their moment to prove that they are important, that they do have a purpose, and that they cannot just be eliminated and forgotten."

"Kind of like you," said Rosalina softly, and the words hit Punching Crab like a charging rhino. After all, Punch might, or might not, ever be a spirit animal, but either way he could still have a purpose.

"These animals are doing their part," said Brody. "Now we need to do ours. We need to get Jake and Grammy, and then find a way into Sarraka, and we can't do it without you."

Punch nodded. "You make a good point," he said, looking at Brody and then Rosalina. "But we still have a big problem," he added. "I have no idea how to get into Sarraka."

"There's always a way," said Brody, looking around for

another way to bust Punching Crab out of his cell. "You taught me that. You'll figure it out. We'll figure it out together."

Punch stopped rolling the golden acorn and simply squeezed it tight. "I don't think you get it," he said. "Do you know how long Felonious was trying to get into Sarraka? He had pages and pages of research. He kept that research in a binder that he hid at the bottom of the lake where he lived. He used to tell me that all the answers were in that binder, and if I ever needed to get into Sarraka, the best place to start was that binder. He said that binder at the bottom of the lake was the key to everything, and if I were ever desperate, I shouldn't panic or give up. I should just think of this golden acorn, find that binder, and it would provide the answers. So like I said," Punch concluded with a shrug, "even if we did get out of here alive, I wouldn't know where to start."

Brody rolled his eyes at Rosalina, who shook her head and smiled back. He looked Punching Crab right in the eye and said . . . well, it didn't really matter what Brody said. The important part was that when Brody looked Punch right in the eye, Punch looked back, and that's when he forgot about his doubt and focused on the magic. He stared at Brody's right eye and then the left, glancing back and forth again and again just to make sure what he saw was real.

"Your eye," Punch said, rolling the golden acorn faster and faster. He motioned for Brody to move closer. "You have the eye of the Akaway." The light inside Punch's spirit seemed to snap back on as he sat back on his shell and whispered, "Tell me what you see."

chapter 15
Ultimate Nature Quest

A sharp burst of light filled the sky, and for just an instant everything was right in Sarraka. The Akaway was home. She allowed herself a moment to soak in the air and the auras that instantly fueled her spirit. Then she rested her paw on the rich Sarraka soil and listened to the rhythms of the land flowing through the ground.

THUMP, thump, thump, thump.

It was those rhythms that told the Akaway everything she needed to know. That the Scallywaggers had reached the Pleasant Tree. That Felonious and Uncle Skeeta were preparing Rudy for the difficult climb that lay ahead. And that time was not on her side.

In an instant, the Akaway was gone, speeding through the long grass, across the open fields, and over the rolling hills in a final attempt to save the world she loved. At the same time, Felonious was preparing Rudy for the most important tree climb of his young life.

"We need to get you up there as soon as possible," said Felonious, as if he could feel rhythms as well.

"Why? What's going on?" asked Rudy. "Where did that bright light come from?"

"The Akaway," answered Felonious, rushing Rudy to the base of the tree. "Now we need you to climb like you've never climbed before."

A combination of excitement and stress swept over Rudy's body as he stood toe-to-trunk with the tree that meant so much to a magical world. He guessed that it stood hundreds of feet in the air, or as tall as the Statue of Liberty standing on the shoulders of the Statue of Liberty.

"Just think of this as an awesome new video game," suggested Uncle Skeeta. "The hero teams with nature to take over the world. And that's what we're going to do."

"We can call it Nature Quest," proposed Rudy.

"Not bad," replied Uncle Skeeta with a thoughtful nod. "But how about we go a little further—X-treme Nature Quest. Remember, everything sounds better with an Ultimate or an *X* in front of it."

Rudy nodded, allowing the powers of Sarraka and the inspiration from Uncle Skeeta to fill his spirit as he started to climb with speed and purpose. His mind was clear, and his emotions were controlled as he scaled the trunk and leaped from branch to branch with an agility and grace that surprised even himself.

Of course, the Pleasant Tree was not meant for climbing—in fact, just the opposite. Its branches and bark were there to protect the Rock of Sarraka, not make it easier to capture. One time Rudy's foot was stuck in a gap between two branches, and he had to leave his shoe behind to escape. A few moments later, Rudy reached for a branch that wasn't there—it was just an illusion that Rudy figured out when he finally started seeing with his third eye. There were plenty of scrapes and scratches, but every time Rudy fell or slipped or succumbed to the natural obstacles of the tree that might not have been so pleasant, it only made him more determined to right himself and keep going.

In what seemed like record time, Rudy was only a few feet away from the top. Hanging on to a branch with his left hand, he swung back and forth until his momentum allowed him to reach another limb with his right hand. Dangling high above the air, Rudy then used both hands to pull himself up like a chimpanzee. He took a deep breath and jumped to the final branch—and that's where he saw the Rock.

At first, it appeared like any other rock—dirty, gray, and about the size of a softball—but being so close to something so important, Rudy understood that looks really didn't matter. It was what was on the inside that counted. Once again, he controlled his emotions, something that almost nobody could do in the presence of something so powerful. That was the focus that made Rudy special. He could see things other people couldn't.

A confident smile appeared on his face. He wished Brody were there, watching the power shift right in front of his own eyes. It would have made the victory more special. But never mind. Rudy looked down at Felonious and Uncle Skeeta and yelled, "I almost have it."

Then he reached out his right arm, opened his hand wide and strong around the rock, and squeezed. But when he opened his hand, it was empty.

The Split

Felonious and Uncle Skeeta waited patiently as Rudy experienced several emotions like shock, frustration, and utter confusion before climbing down the Pleasant Tree slowly and quietly.

"It looks like we're going to have to do this the hard way," Felonious sighed, patting Rudy on the shoulder.

"You mean that was the easy way?" snapped Rudy, flashing his hands and knees, which were covered in just the right amount of blood. Then suddenly, he felt calm, as if the challenge of climbing such an extraordinary tree was worthwhile, even if it wasn't a total success. The energy of Sarraka was just starting to fill Rudy's spirit. He could feel his senses expand and his mind connect. Was this what Brody felt like? Rudy wanted more, and he was prepared to do anything to get it.

Felonious gathered a small feast of bananas, coconuts, and sunflower seeds, all thanks to the nature around him. Rudy and Uncle Skeeta would need the energy. While they ate, Felonious scooped up a golden acorn that lay in a nest at the base of the tree and placed it in his finny pack—they just might need that as well. Then he shifted his attention to an odd-looking watch that hung from his belt. Felonious carefully studied the face of the watch before turning it toward Rudy and Uncle Skeeta.

"It's called a vitality meter," explained Felonious, which made sense, because vitality means "life," and this device measured the seismic waves, barometric pressure, and every other important factor to determine exactly how much life was left in Sarraka. "Time is on our side," said Felonious, flashing the vitality meter toward Rudy and Uncle Skeeta. "The needle is safely in the green zone on the right, nowhere near the red danger zone over here," Felonious said, pointing to the left.

"That's great," said Uncle Skeeta dismissively, meaning

he was much more interested in what just happened on the Pleasant Tree. "Where did that rock go?"

It was a reasonable question, and Felonious was about to answer, but just at that instant, he felt something strange sweeping through his spirit. An empty feeling of nothingness that had no place in Sarraka. Felonious quickly scanned the area, but of course, he saw nothing.

Felonious looked to Uncle Skeeka and Rudy, who clearly didn't feel anything odd. So Felonious took five deep breaths to clear his mind before telling the story about how the Rock of Sarraka could be there one second and gone the next.

It turned out that when the Akaway returned to Sarraka, she didn't have time to get to the Pleasant Tree. The Scallywaggers had too big of a head start. But she did have time to travel to a very special cave known as the Aka Lair, where all the key elements of Sarraka—fire, water, and air—converged, or came together, into one concentrated area.

"When the Akaway is home in the Aka Lair, she is totally connected to Sarraka," said Felonious. "And she used that connection to activate the Split." Felonious knew the next question, so he quickly added, "The Split is a burst of light from the sky that shattered the Rock of Sarraka just in the nick of time."

"What do you mean, 'shattered'?" asked Rudy. "Why would the Akaway want to shatter the Rock of Sarraka?"

"To protect it," guessed Uncle Skeeta, and he was right. "So where is the rock now?" he asked Felonious. "Back in the Aka Lair?"

"If only it were that easy," replied Felonious. "No. The Rock of Sarraka was shattered into three equal pieces—one representing fire, one representing water, and the last, and most important one, representing air. The three jagged rocks are hidden in the three furthest regions of Sarraka." Felonious shook his head and shrugged. "They're impossible to find." Then he grinned and added, "And we're going to find them."

Felonious waited just long enough to build a little suspense before shifting his gaze to Rudy. "This is something you'll be particularly interested in knowing," said Felonious, and Rudy's eyes widened. "Each time we collect a piece of the rock, the balance of power will shift. That means that with each rock, a third of the power of the Akaway will transfer."

"Transfer from where? To where?" asked Rudy, trying to hold back the mischievous grin on his face, because he already knew the answer. Still it felt good to hear Felonious confirm, "From Brody Boondoggle to you."

Now the grin turned into a massive smile that was almost too big for Rudy's face. Not only would tracking down these rocks make Rudy stronger, but it would also make Brody Boondoggle weaker. Sarraka really was making his dreams come true.

"So if these rocks are impossible to find, how are we going to find them?" asked Uncle Skeeta.

"Well, I hoped this wouldn't happen," said Felonious, reaching into his finny pack. "But I prepared just in case it did." He pulled out a device a little bigger than a cell phone.

"The Rock Tracker," Felonious announced, describing the only instrument in the universe that could pick up the exact wavelengths coming from the Rock of Sarraka. "Something I was trusted with many years ago. I had a feeling it might come in handy one day, so I just kind of hung on to it, just in case."

"How about we call it the Ultimate Rock Tracker?" suggested Rudy.

"Now you're getting it," said Uncle Skeeta with a proud smile as he pulled Rudy close and gave him a hug. "It's all about finding ways to adapt, give yourself options, make sure you win no matter what," and he knew Rudy was inhaling his words like a panda, which can spend as much as half of the day consuming food.

"He's right," said Felonious. "If we had captured the rock at the Pleasant Tree, we would have the power. But the Akaway made her move. No worries. Now we'll make ours, and we'll still win."

Uncle Skeeta thought for a moment before turning to Felonious. "What about the Akaway?" he said. "This is her home turf, and she's connected. She probably knows exactly where the rocks are hidden. Will we even stand a chance?"

Felonious just shook his head. "Maybe I didn't explain myself properly," he said. "Do you realize how much energy it takes to break the Rock of Sarraka? The Akaway sacrificed everything she had to pull off the Split. Very annoying, but completely predictable. So yes, she is connected, and yes, she probably is the Ultimate Rock Tracker. But she has nothing left. Sarraka is at its most vulnerable right now. It'll take time for the Akaway to recover, and by then, we'll have what we came for."

Too Quiet

Punch grabbed a pile of magazines that he had stolen from the prison library—stealing was a bad habit that he had learned from a few of his fellow inmates. He spread the magazines on his cot and then covered them with the blanket, so, at first glance, it would appear that he was dreaming, which made sense because that's what Punch spent most of his time doing.

"The Akaway needs us," said Punch. "We're out of here."

"I like the confidence," said Brody. "But how? Those bars don't budge."

Punch didn't answer. Instead, he just walked up to the bars, took a deep breath, and held it so his chest was as thin as possible. Then he turned sideways and slid right through the space between the bars. He even had room to spare.

"You gotta be kidding me," said Brody. "You could have just walked out the entire time?"

"I wanted to give you a chance to break me out," he said, giving Brody a big hug. "That was your plan, right?"

"Classic El Pantsing Crab," whispered Rosalina, as she carefully removed the mirrors from the security cameras.

"That reminds me," whispered Brody, "why do they call you El Pantsing Crab?"

Punch was about to answer when Rosalina interrupted. "We don't have time for any more stories right now. It's been quiet," Rosalina added. "Too quiet. *Mi abuela* is up to something."

"Maybe your *abuela* is not as smart as you think," suggested Brody.

"She's smarter," said Rosalina, as she reconsidered the escape route, meaning she came up with a new plan to rescue Jake and Grammy.

Rosalina directed Brody and Punch outside the room that held Punch's cell. Just as Rosalina suspected, they could hear what sounded like two guards running on the floor just above, and Rosalina knew they didn't have much time. Still, she was calm and calculating.

"Which way?" asked Punch, who was neither calm *nor* calculating. "We have to get out of here before the guards come."

Rosalina took a brief moment to study her surroundings. At the end of the long hallway, she noticed a small maintenance closet that held brooms and buckets and everything else you would need to make sure a prison was nice and clean, just as La Tarántula liked it.

"Maybe we don't," she said with a sly grin. "I have a different idea."

Rosalina dropped to her knees and opened the Hoodster. She quickly removed a small container of coconut oil and instructed Brody and Punch to spread the slippery substance all over the hallway floor. "Myles and I used to pull this prank all the time," she bragged. "Make sure to leave a small, clean space in front of the closet. That's where you guys will wait."

Then she handed Punch an object that looked like a horseshoe. "It's a magnet," Rosalina explained. She flipped open a small lever on the side. "A very powerful magnet with an aiming device."

While explaining the details of her plan, Rosalina pulled an ultra-thin piece of fishing wire, a hammer, and two nails from the Hoodster. Moments later, the fishing wire was secured tightly across the entrance to the hallway about a foot off the ground.

"You ready?" Rosalina asked, as the patter from the guards grew louder. Brody and Punch finished covering the floor with coconut oil and nodded. "Then here we go," said Rosalina. She took a deep breath and started running away from Brody, around the corner, and toward the sound of the guards. Seconds later, she was sprinting back—only this time, two guards were following right behind.

Rosalina ran as fast as she could, but the guards were gaining. When they saw Brody at the end of the hallway, it only made them run faster, and they were just about to grab Rosalina when she dove headfirst over the wire on the floor and started sliding on the world's best coconut oil slip-n-slide. The guards didn't need to dive. With no time to react or slow down, they tripped on the wire and began sliding as well.

"¡Ahhhhh!" the guards yelled, flapping around on their stomachs.

At that moment, Brody opened the closet door and waited with Punch. They each had a job to do, and now was the time to do it.

Brody went first. While the guards were sliding wildly out of control, Rosalina was sliding with grace, her arms stretched out in front. Brody concentrated on a meerkat, which relies on complete and utter trust for survival, and right now, he knew Rosalina was trusting him to make the most important catch of his life.

He braced himself with one arm and stretched out the other. Just before Rosalina reached the closet, she and Brody clasped hands and Brody pulled her to safety.

The guards, on the other hand, did not have the loyalty of the meerkats to save them. What they did have were the keys to the jail cell attached to their belts, and Rosalina knew it. That's why she gave Punch the magnet, which he aimed at the metal keys and held on as tight as he could. The guards slid into the closet, but the keys stayed with Punch, who quickly closed and locked the closet door.

"Just like I said," smiled Punching Crab, dangling the keys in his claws like a prize. "Piece of cake."

"More guards will be coming soon," said Rosalina. "We have to go."

"Can't we just enjoy the moment for a moment?" asked Punch. "There's a lot going on here."

Rosalina waited for a beat. "There," she said. "Now the moment is over. Follow me."

Capture
the Crab

Rosalina, Punching Crab, and Brody Boondoggle started sprinting faster and faster, skillfully avoiding the cameras that surveyed almost every inch of the prison. They dashed through a series of trapdoors and scampered through the laundry facility, hiding in the steam from the dryers. They climbed the pipes over the high-security cellblock, where all the most dangerous criminals lived, and crawled across the pipes in the ceiling.

Punch waved to his fellow prisoners, who smiled back and cheered quietly, because they understood some crabs were meant to fly.

Finally, they scurried through the corridor and into

the elaborate tunnel system that ended at the holding cell that contained Jake, Grammy, and Tackle.

"I think you have been in here long enough," said Rosalina with a charming grin. "How about we get you out of here?"

Rosalina fumbled with the keys, while Brody quickly explained who this new girl was and why she was unlocking the door to their freedom.

"Takes some guts to go against La Tarántula," Jake said to Rosalina when she finally opened the door to the cell. "Even if she is your grandmother." Rosalina smiled. Jake turned to Punch, who gave Jake a big hug. A few seconds later, Punch handed Jake the "Hair Like a Rock Star" gel he had stolen from Jake's back pocket without even thinking. "I'm trying to quit stealing," Punching Crab shrugged.

"No problem," said Jake with a wink. "It's just good to know you're okay. It couldn't have been easy being locked away." Finally, he looked at Brody. "Way to almost blow it for everyone. Where have you been?"

"Sorry. I was going to call, but I didn't have a *cell* phone," Brody answered sarcastically. "And don't forget who just rescued you."

"What do you want, a cookie?" asked Jake, nudging Brody with his shoulder. Brody pushed him back, which only caused a slight movement. It was getting frustrating that his powers didn't have nearly the same effect when he was fighting his big brother.

"And where was the distraction?" said Brody, who just had to continue the argument. "I thought you were supposed to make sure the coast was clear. I've been chased like a warthog since I got here."

"Toughen up," said Jake, and Brody glanced at Punching Crab as if to say, "I told you so." Punch was still looking for the cookie.

"I hate to break this up," Rosalina interjected, "but we have to get out of here." She looked to Grammy, who stood up slowly and waited in the cell with her arms wide open. Brody rolled his eyes. "We don't have time for this, Grammy," he said, but he knew that Grammy believed there was always time for a hug, so that's what he gave her.

Brody officially introduced Rosalina, and, of course, Grammy insisted on a hug from her as well. It was the nicest hug Rosalina could remember in a long time, and she didn't let go until Brody finally pulled them apart.

"Okay, let's stay focused," said Brody, as Tackle licked his face. "We need a new escape route."

"I'm pretty sure there's something behind this wall," said Jake. "Unfortunately, we can't find a way to break through."

Rosalina grabbed the map from her Hoodster and compared it with the location in the cell. "You're right," she said, moments later. "There's a hidden passage right here."

Before Jake could ask about how to open the passage, Rosalina had already started running her fingers over the bricks on the opposite side of the cell until she found the spot that matched the one on the map. She reached into the Hoodster and removed a solid wooden mallet, which she used to knock firmly on the brick. The brick didn't move, but the vibrations from the pounding released the latch that opened a secret passage directly where Jake and Grammy were scratching away.

Without a moment to lose, Rosalina led everyone out of the holding cell and through a maze of tunnels that ended in a small but comfortable-looking bathroom, complete with bright blue tiles on the floor and a big white tub against the wall.

"Awesome," said Punching Crab. "I've had to go for a while. Could you guys excuse me?"

"You're going to have to hold it a little longer," said Rosalina. "This is not an ordinary bathroom." Rosalina pushed the drain in the bottom of the bathtub and pulled. The entire tub slid a few feet back, revealing an escape hatch. "It's connected to a tunnel system that leads to a passageway to the roof," explained Rosalina.

"Why the roof?" asked Jake.

"Because that's how we escape," smiled Rosalina as she opened the hatch. Brody and Punching Crab beamed, and Tackle licked Rosalina's face. Grammy was still trying to figure out what was so important about a cabbageway named Ruth.

Then they climbed through the tunnels to the passageway and up a slanted ladder step-by-step to the top of the prison. In a single-file line, they tiptoed across the giant roof as softly as flies landing in a spider's web until they reached the perfect spot for their escape. Just a few moments later, their smiles faded, because they knew exactly how those flies felt. They couldn't move a muscle. They had been caught by La Tarántula.

Gracias for Everything

Brody Boondoggle was so close to getting away that he could almost hear the waves from the Pacific Ocean calling to him, encouraging him to try harder to break free from the sticky web-like substance that now trapped him and the rest of his friends. He struggled briefly, but it was obvious to anyone with even a little common sense that struggling to escape only made it worse.

"The trick is to struggle as much as you can," whispered Punching Crab, as he attempted to kick and punch his way free. But the more he struggled, the more stuck he became.

All the while, Brody noticed that Rosalina seemed perfectly calm. "Remember my promise," Rosalina said, as her mind raced with possibilities. "I'm going to get you out of here." And there was something about her energy —a unique ability to remain composed in a storm of chaos—that made Brody believe her, without a doubt.

A few moments later, Rosalina turned to Punch. "Do you still have that magnet I gave you?"

Punching Crab was too terrified to think clearly, so he just said the first thing that came to his mind: "Laga, laga, laga."

Before Rosalina could ask again, Jake pointed to the bottom of Punch's shell. "Is that it?" he asked. Rosalina nodded, and Jake knew what to do next. The agility and courage of the ocelot would not be much help, so Jake focused on its ability to concentrate and control its body with precision. And when he did, he was able to slide to the right and wiggle his fingers just enough to secure the magnet.

From there, Jake did exactly as Rosalina instructed. He aimed the high-powered magnet at the side zipper on the Hoodster and pulled down just enough to open the compartment. Then he adjusted the magnet slightly and removed a long, straight metal rod with a small, sharp hook on the end. Jake used the magnet to carefully guide the instrument through the air until it landed in Rosalina's left hand. Myles had spent a long time observing La Tarántula, and he clearly had prepared Rosalina for everything.

Without hesitation, Rosalina placed the hook in position and moved her arm strategically up and down three times in a smooth fluid motion—whoosh, whoosh, whoosh—slicing the web as easily as if she were unzipping a jacket.

She made the same motion to free Jake, Brody, Punch, Grammy, and Tackle—whoosh, whoosh, whoosh—but whatever pride Rosalina might have been feeling quickly faded when a tall, strong figure emerged from the door on the other side of the roof.

"¡Deténganse!" La Tarántula yelled. "Give up now before it is too late."

It's never too late, Brody thought to himself, but he actually believed it when he heard Rosalina whisper, "Don't worry. It's never too late."

There was a reason Rosalina had taken everyone to this spot on the roof. It was the exact place Myles had told her to go, the place that was set up for the perfect escape. And even though La Tarántula was loud and mean and pretty scary to everyone but Grammy, who offered a warm wave, she was still all the way on the other side of the giant roof.

So Rosalina did not freeze. Instead, she did just as she and Myles had practiced so many times. She removed a long pole from the railing and attached the metal loop in the middle to a wire that ran from the top of the roof to the beach where Brody had first entered the prison. The same beach where an escape boat was now waiting, just like Grammy and Brody had planned.

"I know you dream about zip lines," Rosalina nodded to Brody. "Let me know what you think of this one." Tackle jumped into Jake's arms, and they all grabbed hold of the bar, safely securing their hands in the straps that were already there.

"Just one more thing," said Rosalina. She glanced over her shoulder and saw La Tarántula running with two guards close behind. Rosalina predicted that they had less than a minute, which was plenty of time to peel off the Hoodster and hand it to Brody.

"It's all yours," she said with a smile. "Always keep it close."

Brody glanced at the Hoodster and then back at Rosalina. "You're not making any sense," said Brody. "There's no way in a million years we're leaving without you."

"Don't worry," replied Rosalina, lifting the necklace from her chest. "I'm not alone."

Before Brody could respond, Rosalina turned around, scooped up the sticky web that was still on the ground, and ran straight for La Tarántula and the guards. Brody immediately knew what Rosalina was thinking. She was going to keep her promise. She was going to make sure Brody and his friends made it out of the prison, even if it meant she never would.

Brody watched as Rosalina slid down on her side and wrapped the web around the guards' legs. The guards didn't fall, and La Tarántula only slowed briefly, but that was enough.

"Go," yelled Rosalina. "Now."

Rosalina's sacrifice provided just enough extra time for Brody to slip the Hoodster over his shoulders and the hood over his head and swiftly climb onto the ledge of the prison.

"*Gracias*, for everything," Brody mouthed to Rosalina, which didn't seem like nearly enough thanks, considering all they had been through together.

La Tarántula shouted something else in Spanish, but it was too late. She could only watch as Brody, Jake, Grammy, Punch, and Tackle jumped off the roof and flew through the air as carefree as a family of passenger pigeons.

And as the sun started to rise over the horizon, it was a brand-new day in more ways than one. When they landed safely on the soft, white beach, everyone boarded the escape boat and settled in for the start of a long journey home. They talked very little except to say things like, "I don't ever want to go back to prison," or "What does the golden acorn do?" or "I used to think that the carpool lane was for cars that had actual pools."

Part II
The Fake Out

And Then It Wasn't

Brody Boondoggle thought of a hummingbird and hovered in the air high above Sarraka. The spirit-animal world was everything he dreamed it would be. The colors were bright, the air was clean, and the possibilities were endless. It was peaceful and perfect.

And then it wasn't.

Brody's smile faded as everything changed right before his eyes. A dark smoke polluted the air. Trees crashed to the ground. Lakes and streams were sucked dry. Flowers and grass started to wilt and fade.

Brody tried to run, but he couldn't move his legs. He tried to yell, but the words wouldn't come. He took five deep breaths to regain his strength, but it was too late. He was getting sucked in by a nothingness that was destroying everything he embraced.

He tried to pull free with the might of a hippopotamus, a moose, even the tiny leaf-cutter ant, which can carry as much as 50 times its own body weight in its jaws—which would be like you or me lifting a hippopotamus or a moose with our teeth. But it wasn't enough. He was falling faster and faster. This was the end of Brody, of Sarraka, of everything.

And then it wasn't.

chapter 21

The Good in Bad Dreams

"Wake up."

Brody felt a hand on his shoulder, and then he heard the words again.

"Wake up."

His heart was racing as he opened his eyes and saw the dark outline of a girl sitting on the side of his bed staring down at him.

"You were dreaming," he heard the girl say. She had long dark hair and glasses.

Maybe I still am, Brody thought to himself. He blinked a few more times, waiting for his eyes to adjust from the sun that was sneaking in through the holes in the shades.

"Rosalina?" he asked in disbelief.

Rosalina flashed a simple smile, and, for a brief moment, Brody was a little lost, staring into her deep blue eyes, which reminded him of the ocean—filled with so much energy and emotion and incredible possibilities.

"Let's go," she said with the excitement of someone who was ready for whatever adventure lay ahead. "We have things to do. Worlds to save. No time to waste."

It had been only five days since Brody had returned from Mexico, and between the journey back home and the preparations for what was still to come, he was getting closer to embracing that excitement, too.

"But how did you get away? How did you find me?" Brody asked, not quite fully awake. Then his mind snapped into full awareness mode as he barked the most important question of all, "Where is La Tarántula?"

Before Rosalina could answer, Brody jumped from his bed and peeked out the window from behind the shade. Adrenaline shot through his body when he saw a shadow coming from around the corner. At that point, he wouldn't have been surprised if it had been La Tarántula sneaking up the driveway, ready to strike.

"Thank you," Brody said after a huge exhale. The shadow was not a spider. It was a badger. His friend Alec, was walking into the backyard to meet Punching Crab, Jake, Tackle, and Grammy, who were sitting peacefully in the middle of a pink blanket. Ever since Brody's birthday party, Alec simply appeared whenever the badger in him smelled action.

Brody watched Punching Crab give Alec a huge hug. He chuckled a few seconds later when Punching Crab returned the small container of extra-strength "Breath So Bad" mouthwash he stole from Alec's back pocket.

Brody turned back to Rosalina, who couldn't help but stare and smirk.

"What?" said Brody, turning his head all around to see what was so funny.

When he finally realized the inspiration for Rosalina's stare—Brody was wearing only an old pair of red boxer shorts covered in purple polka dots—Brody's face turned as red as the shorts, and he dashed into his closet to change. There was an awkward silence before Rosalina finally blurted, "I assume you're wondering how I got here?"

"You assume correct," said Brody, emerging from the

closet wearing navy blue cargo shorts and a gray T-shirt.

Rosalina explained that after Brody zip-lined off the roof, La Tarántula and the guards immediately ran down the stairs in hot pursuit, meaning they were completely focused on stopping Brody before he got on the boat. When they were too late, La Tarántula was so angry that she stormed off down the beach.

"It's one of the few times I've seen her so distracted," said Rosalina. "She completely forgot that I was still on the roof."

Almost an hour later, Rosalina saw La Tarántula re-enter the prison and realized the beach was clear of the guards. "I had two choices," Rosalina said. "Go back to my room and wait to feel the wrath of La Tarántula. Or zip-line down to the beach and sneak onto the prison supply boat that was on its way."

It seemed like an easy choice at first. But then the doubt started to form deep in Rosalina's belly and carry through her body. She was nervous and scared, in the same way she was the day Myles left.

"And that's how I knew I had to jump," Rosalina said with pride. "Zip-lining down from the top of the prison was the greatest feeling of my life. It's the first time I truly knew how it felt to be free."

Brody stared at Rosalina almost apologetically, meaning part of him felt proud of the adventures that, thanks to Grammy, were just a part of his everyday life, and another part felt a little guilty because he never considered that other kids didn't have the same chances.

"So how did you find me?" he asked. Rosalina picked up the dark gray Hoodster with all the zippers and pockets and the big, bold letters AIP.

"It comes with a global tracking system," said Rosalina. "That's why I wanted you to keep it close. I took a boat to a bus, and here I am."

Rosalina paused and quickly changed the subject. "That dream you were having seemed pretty intense. You were tossing and turning and mumbling about a nothingness." She thought for a moment. "What did you see?"

Brody took a deep breath and told Rosalina all about the images in his dreams that continued to haunt him, like a cruel new chapter of the same story, playing over and over in his head. It was a constant reminder of his strong connection to Sarraka and just how far away he truly was.

"Something bad is looming," said Brody. "I don't know what it is or what it wants, but it's coming. I can feel it."

Rosalina could sense the seriousness in Brody's tone, so she tried to see things in a different way. "I actually like bad dreams the most," Rosalina said with a nod.

"Why would you like bad dreams?" Brody asked.

"Think about it," said Rosalina. "If you're having a really good dream, like you have super speed or you can travel through time, and then you wake up and realize that it's just a dream, you're totally bummed. But if you're having a bad dream, like you didn't study for a huge test or a nothingness is taking over the land you love, and then you wake up, you're totally psyched, because you know it was just a dream."

"You make an interesting point," Brody nodded, as he searched the pile of clothes on the floor before finding a single sock. He held it to his nose and made a nasty face, then put it on.

"Are you sure you know what you're doing?" Brody asked, reaching for another sock. "It's going to be a real nightmare when your grandmother finds you. And she will find you," he cautioned. "I learned that from you."

Rosalina shook her head and thought for a few seconds, trying to figure out exactly how to respond.

"You know what I dream of?" she finally said.

"Pirates?" answered Brody.

"Sometimes," admitted Rosalina. "But mostly, it's the stars. Myles and I loved the stars," she continued. "He believed that they were the one thing that connected us all. I can sometimes see a few of them outside my window, but my grandmother forbids me to go out onto the balcony to see more. She says I'd be an easy target. And just a few stars are not enough. I want to see an endless sea of stars."

"Like the painting on your wall," suggested Brody.

"Exactly like the painting," said Rosalina. "Myles described that picture to me, and I painted it. He said it came from his dreams. I looked at it every night and dreamt that someday I was going to see that many stars. And when that happens, and I see all those stars staring back down at me, well, then I guess I will believe what Myles always told me. That anything is possible."

Anything is possible, Brody said to himself as if he could see the words written in his mind. He studied those words and suddenly everything made sense.

"Anything is possible," Brody repeated aloud. "Is that what AIP stands for?"

Rosalina nodded. "Myles never wanted me to forget," she confirmed.

Brody nodded back, and there was another awkward moment that Brody interrupted by asking, "Where do you think Myles is right now?"

"Knowing Myles," Rosalina answered almost immediately, "exactly where he was meant to be."

Myles

The Akaway lay weak and weary in the Aka Lair. She knew what would happen if she activated the Split—her strength would be tested, her energy absorbed—and it was still an easy decision. The rock that was so important to the life of Sarraka was now split into three equal pieces and scattered throughout the land. The little energy the Akaway had left was being used to send assistance to Brody in the form of dreams, visions, and extinct animals, which were no longer in his world but were still willing to help.

"Can I help?"

The question came from a voice so quiet even the

Akaway could barely hear it. But that made sense, because the creature who asked it was a little quiet as well—at least until you got to know him. The Akaway smiled because her instincts told her that this creature belonged in Sarraka, and she always trusted her instincts.

"What's your name?"

"Myles," the voice whispered back.

"That's a great name," said the Akaway in the special way an Akaway communicates, which is a voice you hear deep inside your spirit. "Why don't you come out from behind that tree and join me?"

A medium-sized animal with light brown fur covering its body from the tips of its large, pointed ears to its fluffy, bushy tail slowly moved a few steps out of the shadows of the tree.

"You're a swift fox," nodded the Akaway with just a little sadness, because she knew Myles was an extremely rare kind of swift fox who had been extinct for a very long time. And Myles shrugged as if to say, "I have been my whole life."

"So tell me, Myles," the Akaway continued. "How did you find this place?"

Myles paused, thought for a moment, and responded that he didn't find Sarraka, Sarraka found him. He told the Akaway that for the longest time, he had been living in a Mexican prison with a girl who was special and different and good.

Even so, deep down, Myles knew the prison was no place for a swift fox, which is known for being smart, cunning, and eager to move around and explore new areas. So when the time was right, Myles left.

Myles was exploring in the woods on the same day as Brody Boondoggle's birthday party, and he saw Brody and his friends just as they entered the Sequestered Spring. His instincts told him there was something special and different and good about Brody as well, so Myles decided to take a detour from his own journey and follow Brody's instead.

When the portal to Sarraka opened, and everyone was distracted by the confrontation between Uncle Skeeta, Felonious Fish, Brody, and Jake, Myles took a second detour and jumped through the portal. In that moment, Myles knew that he was home. And, in the same way as his fellow animals, Myles felt a desire to help just when

Sarraka needed it most.

"Instincts are a great gift we all have," said the Akaway. "I'm glad you trusted yours."

Myles smiled and listened to his instincts again. Right now they were telling him that the Akaway was tired. So he stood up, walked out of the cave, and several moments later returned with a coconut full of fresh milk, which he carefully placed next to the Akaway. Then Myles sat down on a nearby log, and that's where he remained for the perfect amount of time.

Myles came back the next day and the day after that and the day after that—each time bringing water, berries, and other nourishing foods to help the Akaway recover as much as possible.

Days turned to weeks, and the quantity of conversation gradually increased, meaning not only was Myles willing to share a few more details about himself—his favorite color was blue, he once stole all of his sister's Halloween candy (he would do it again), and if he could have only one wish, it would be for it to rain chocolate—but he felt comfortable enough to ask the Akaway a few questions as well.

"What will happen if Rudy, Uncle Skeeta, and Felonious collect the three pieces of the Rock of Sarraka?"

"Kids will never connect with their spirit animals again."

"Why doesn't someone else get the rocks before they do?"

"It doesn't work that way. Not just anyone can handle those rocks. It takes a person with very special powers. Brody Boondoggle has the power. And, unfortunately, so does Rudy."

"What if someone without the power tries?"

"It would be a tremendous risk. The connection with their spirit animal would be severely injured, and probably worse."

Myles thought for a moment, considering all this new information, and realized this was his chance to help. This was the reason he was here. "We have to hold them off as long as possible," said Myles with confidence. "That's something I can do."

"I love your spirit," said the Akaway, who saw something special in Myles. So even though the Akaway was still weak, she found the strength to do what she was born to do. And just like that, things instantly froze. The Akaway's body felt warm, but right. She took a deep breath, and a few seconds later, everything moved in super slow motion.

THUMP, thump, thump, thump.

The beat seemed to be coming from two places: in the Akaway's own chest and directly in front of her. The beats were synchronized. Rhythmical. Perfect.

When the Akaway looked up, the swift fox was gone. And in its place was a 12-year-old boy with braces and glasses. That's when Myles first felt this new energy, and it felt right. So did the pendant hanging around his neck, and Myles knew this was exactly what he needed for this important adventure.

"Just remember," warned the Akaway, "Felonious is smart. Uncle Skeeta is creative, and Rudy is getting more powerful every day. And they don't play by the rules."

"Then it will be fair," said Myles, a devious smile forming on his face as he placed his Hoodster over his shoulders and a dark hood over his head. "Because neither do I."

SWEEPE

Rosalina had no idea what to expect when she repeated her story to Jake, Punching Crab, Alec, and, especially, Grammy. How much trouble would she be in? Would she be allowed to continue the adventure? Would she be sent back home? But her nerves immediately melted away as Grammy just smiled, gave her a heartfelt hug, and said, "Everything will be just fine." And, in a way, just hearing Grammy say those words made everyone else feel better, too.

After all, for the first time in a long time, they had a little momentum, which basically meant things were going their way. It started when they found Punching

Crab and broke him out of prison. When they returned home, Brody, Jake, Tackle, and Punch hiked to the pond where Felonious lived, and it took Punch only thirteen tries to remember exactly where to find Felonious' binder full of research.

That gave Jake the chance to pull the second all-nighter of his life, and, after organizing the notes, studying the diagrams, and cross-referencing the theories, everyone congratulated him, because now they were dangerously close to figuring out where to go next.

"It was a total team effort," responded Jake. "Would have been lost without you," he said to Punch. "And thanks for missing summer school to help us out," he told Alec.

"It's the least I could do," Alec replied. "Just don't tell my parents."

"As for you," he said to Brody, "well, luckily, we have Rosalina." Jake winked at Rosalina and promised, "You'll fit right into SWEEPE."

Rosalina glanced curiously at Brody. "It's what we call our group," he explained. "I know it doesn't really make much sense. We just kind of like it."

Rosalina smiled back. "I like it, too."

"El desayuno está en sus calzoncillos," Grammy interrupted, carrying a large tray of food from the house. Rosalina giggled and politely explained that Grammy had said, "Breakfast is in your underpants."

"Strange. That's not the best place for breakfast," smiled Grammy.

While everyone filled their bellies with Grammy's famous jalapeño scrambled eggs, black beans, green salsa, and avocado, Rosalina offered to help Grammy in her quest to learn Spanish, and since "doing" is the best way to learn, she started by taking the binder full of research and translating the key words into Spanish.

hill. . . *la colina*

dangerous. . . *peligroso*

mountains. . . *las montañas*

endless sea of stars. . . *un infinito mar de estrellas*

Suddenly Rosalina paused. She quickly flipped through the next several pages reviewing the list of locations that Jake had highlighted. Something about the images of nature and geography felt very familiar to Rosalina. And when she turned one more page, suddenly she knew why.

"Yo sé a dónde vamos," she shouted, and then she looked up and repeated, "I know where we're going."

Rosalina passed the binder to Brody, and he immediately understood. The picture in the binder, the one Brody was looking at now, was the same picture on Rosalina's wall—the one with the mountains and stars and a massive gully with a long, narrow bridge high above.

"Can this be true?" Brody asked in amazement.

"It has to be," said Rosalina. "Don't you see? It's all connected."

Brody quickly scanned the page on the opposite side of the picture and saw a place called the Grappling Mountains. "It makes sense," said Brody. "It says here the Grappling Mountains are the best place to look for rocks. Geologists say it's like picking fresh apples off a tree."

"That has to be it," said Rosalina with a confidence that continued to grow. "I can feel it."

"Tienes que confiar en los pelos de tu nariz," said Grammy. She was trying to say, "You have to trust your instincts," and was only slightly embarrassed when Rosalina let her know that she actually said, "You have to trust your nose hairs."

"The question is, how are we going to find the Grappling Mountains?" asked Brody.

"I know every inch of this area," said Alec, who had won first place in the state geography bee even though he failed geography. "And I've never heard of the Grappling Mountains. That means they don't exist."

"Or maybe it's just a big-time secret," said Jake, sliding next to Rosalina. "But secrets are like pet squirrels," he said. "It's pretty hard to keep them, even if you really want to."

Paper

When Jake reviewed all the materials that Felonious had left behind, most of it seemed to make perfect sense. The pages were organized, the maps were clear, and the notes were honest. But Jake also noticed three particular sections that were different. One was a different size, one was made of a different material, and one was a different shape. "Different is good," he remembered Grammy saying again and again. So he tagged them all with pink paper clips, because he figured maybe these pages that were different were actually important, even if he didn't know why.

"Hold on a second," said Rosalina, pointing at an orange piece of paper in the shape of a triangle. Jake had tagged that particular page because there were several small rectangular holes cut into the paper. He thought it could be a part of a puzzle, but as hard as he searched, he couldn't find a matching piece. Rosalina did.

She unzipped one of the side compartments on her Hoodster and removed the triangular-shaped book called *Why?* This same book had almost hit Brody and Rosalina in the air vent of the prison. She took the orange piece of paper and carefully laid it on top of the book.

"A perfect fit," announced Rosalina. "You were right, Jake. It is a puzzle."

"The question is, how does it work?" asked Alec. "It seems impossible."

"Anything is possible," answered Rosalina, and Jake glanced at Grammy and rolled his eyes.

"*AIP*," reinforced Brody, and just saying those three letters sparked an idea. He thought for a moment before opening the book to page 26. Before anyone could ask why, Brody simply repeated the letters that were on the painting in Rosalina's room and also on the top of the Hoodster: *AIP*.

"It's a basic code," Brody announced. Each letter corresponded to a number. *A* is the first letter of the alphabet. That's 1. *I* is 9, and *P* is 16. Put it all together and that's 26.

"Myles has been giving you clues all along."

Page 26 was filled with paragraphs and paragraphs about things that might have been interesting but were not as important as a mission. But when Brody covered the page with the orange triangle, the holes in the triangle revealed words, and suddenly, everything made perfect sense.

Find the one place where the water stops flowing,
And you'll be a step closer to where you are going.

Brody repeated the clue as he turned to Alec. "Tell me you know exactly the place that this riddle is talking about?" pleaded Brody.

Alec waited just long enough to build some drama, but his smile finally betrayed him. "I know exactly the place this riddle it talking about," said Alec. And then he announced, "The Baffling Brook. It must be the first step on the way to the Grappling Mountains."

A beautiful combination of excitement and anticipation filled the air, because when you find the first clue to where you're going, you want to get going right away.

SWEEPE agreed to grab all their supplies and meet back at Grammy's in 26 minutes. But before they could get away, Grammy insisted that they gather in front of her home for a quick picture, which she promptly posted on her Instagrammy account.

She noticed that she was now up to four followers.

Same and Different

Blue-and-red flannel pajamas covered in buffalos are great for hanging out at home, but they're not so good for heading out on an adventure, so when Brody noticed what Grammy was wearing, he followed her back into the house.

"Aren't you going to come?" Brody asked. And before Grammy could tell him all the reasons why he wasn't that dumb, and, even if he were, he was probably going to get smarter one day, Brody realized he had spoken too quietly and repeated the question into Grammy's good ear.

"Oh no, I can't join you this time. I'm going to trust my instincts, too. And right now, I have a feeling I'll be needed more here."

Grammy did promise to be there in spirit, which didn't feel as good as if she were there in person, but Brody knew that Grammy always had her reasons. Even so, he continued to quietly follow Grammy as she started preparing food and water and all the other supplies they might need for a journey to a place that had only been seen in a fish's research binder and on a prison wall.

"Is there something you wanted to talk about?" asked Grammy as she searched the closet for the bandanas she and Brody had eco-dyed, using the colors they created from the roots, nuts, and flowers in Grammy's garden.

At first, Brody was going to say, "Not really," but he had learned over the years that Grammy knew "not really" usually meant "yes, really," and if he could find a way to just get the first words out, then talking to someone he trusted usually helped more than he thought.

"You said you have to trust your nose hairs?" said Brody, with a smile. "Well, what if those nose hairs tell you that maybe something not so good is going to happen?"

Grammy motioned for Brody to sit down on the big red chair next to the couch while she retreated to the kitchen.

"Are you having feelings like that?" she asked, returning from the kitchen a few moments later. She handed Brody a frosty mug of raspberry lemonade.

"I don't know, maybe," said Brody. He paused for a moment, as if he were choosing his words carefully. "I mean, I'm having these dreams—dark dreams about Sarraka, like something bad is going to happen. Not to mention there's Felonious and Uncle Skeeta. They're smart," acknowledged Brody. "And then there's Rudy. He used to be my best friend, and now, well, he really doesn't like me very much."

"That might be true," said Grammy, clinking her glass against Brody's as if to make a toast. "But always remember this: You're not alone. You have friends and a big brother to help you, and that might be the most powerful magic there is."

"Jake doesn't believe in magic," Brody grimaced. "He's not helping because he really wants to. He's only helping because you forced him to. Let's face it, he doesn't care about me."

"Oh, my love, brothers can be complicated. You're the perfect combination of the same and different. That can take time to figure out, but it's also what makes the connections so special."

"The only thing special about Jake is that he somehow finds a way to be nice to everyone else and mean to me," countered Brody.

Before Grammy could say, "It's not as bad as you think," Jake rushed into the room with the dishes from breakfast. He kissed Grammy on the cheek and complimented her on the awesome meal before telling Brody he looked like a toady.

Operation Nacho

For someone who was relatively shy until you got to know him, Myles was used to not being noticed. But now, as Myles ducked behind boulders, hid in the brush, and tracked all the movements and methods of the Scallywaggers, he was fully embracing his ability to be "invisible."

All the while, Myles made notes in his journal, writing down different observations, like how Felonious always took a thirty-minute swim in the early evening to keep his mind and body fresh, how Rudy continued to develop spirit-animal skills, like seeing things with his heart instead of his eyes, and how Uncle Skeeta seemed completely focused on learning the ways of Sarraka. "This is going to make a brilliant video game that kids won't be able to resist," he promised, and he was about to explain how when he was interrupted by a loud beeping from the Rock Tracker.

"We're getting close," announced Felonious, holding the Rock Tracker high in the air.

The beeping continued to get stronger as they hiked through parts of Sarraka that even Felonious didn't know existed, until they finally saw a fiery-red mountain in the distance. Myles snuck just a little closer, hiding in the long grass so he could better eavesdrop on the Scallywaggers' conversation.

"A volcano? The rock is in a volcano?" asked Rudy anxiously. At the same time, a small seed of anticipation started to grow in his belly. "Well, let's go. What are we waiting for?"

"All in due time," advised Felonious, holding back his young partner in crime. "The sun has almost set, and you'll need all your strength. We'll camp tonight and volcano tomorrow."

Myles' mind raced as he watched Felonious, Rudy, and Uncle Skeeta create a perfectly functional campsite in almost no time. Picnic tables, chairs, a fire pit. They even had their own dome tents—blue for Felonious, purple for Rudy, and pink for Uncle Skeeta—complete with sleeping bags and air mattresses.

As the sun started to set and the air turned cooler, Uncle Skeeta built a roaring fire and started preparing his famous campfire nachos, while Rudy retreated to his tent to read about volcanoes, and Felonious hiked to a nearby pond for his early evening swim.

You're running out of time, Myles told himself as he watched Uncle Skeeta sprinkle cheese on the nachos before placing them on the fire. The presentation looked delicious, and Myles imagined how excited the Scallywaggers' would be for a good meal after a long day of hiking.

Stay focused, he told himself. *Don't think about nachos.* But Myles thought about the nachos, which turned into a good thing, because it turned into a perfectly devious plan he called Operation Nacho.

Step 1. Get to the nachos.

Myles waited patiently in the shadows, willing Uncle Skeeta to leave the fire, turn his back, or somehow get distracted for just a moment. That's all the time Myles would need. But Uncle Skeeta didn't move. He was too focused on the food, like any good chef.

No problem. Myles reached into his Hoodster, removed a slingshot, and loaded it with a small pebble he found on the ground. He took aim at Uncle Skeeta's tent, then thought for a moment, shifted his target twenty feet to the right, and fired.

"What the. . . ," yelled Rudy, just after the pebble flew into his tent. Seconds later, Uncle Skeeta rushed in, leaving the nachos unguarded.

This was Myles' chance, and he quickly ran to the fire. *Mmmmm, smells good*, he admitted, catching a whiff of the nachos. He could hear Uncle Skeeta and Rudy talking about bees and ants and other logical explanations for the sting in Rudy's leg, and he knew he didn't have long to make his move.

<u>Step 2</u>. *Spice up the nachos.*

Myles reached into his Hoodster and pulled out a black pepper plant and some super-hot red chilies. He looked left, right, and left again, then dumped a king-sized portion of the hot spices all over the nachos.

Step 3. _Escape without a trace._

Myles quickly dashed away, just as Uncle Skeeta emerged from the tent. Unfortunately, it wasn't quite fast enough.

"Hey," yelled Uncle Skeeta. "What are you doing?"

Myles froze behind a tree, hoping that if he believed he was invisible, maybe he would be. But Uncle Skeeta wasn't playing that game.

"I know you're back there," Uncle Skeeta said in a stern tone no kid wants to hear from an adult. Myles took a deep breath and instantly created a Step 4: Act innocent.

"Oh, hey, are you talking to me?" asked Myles, stepping out from behind the trees.

"You're the only one here," Uncle Skeeta replied. "So I guess I am." Uncle Skeeta looked around. "Kind of a strange place for a kid," he added. "You alone?"

Myles thought for a moment. "Yeah, well, I guess you can say I'm lost," he explained calmly. He pulled the hood off his head. "I went for a hike one day in the woods by my house, and I must have taken a wrong turn. The next thing I knew, here I was. But don't worry about me. I can find my own way."

Uncle Skeeta took a step closer to Myles, who tried not to appear frightened, although he was. If Uncle Skeeta was planning to take over Sarraka, who knows what he would do if he caught someone trying to stand in his way?

Uncle Skeeta was only a few feet away from Myles, hovering over him like a moose, which, if spooked, is known to relentlessly stomp its prey. Myles continued to focus on Step 4 and tried to appear calm as Uncle Skeeta glared and stared, as if he were studying everything about this new stranger: his wide eyes, his long hair, the faded blue jeans. Was he a friend or a foe? Was he a spy or worse? Was he here to ruin everything?

Uncle Skeeta took another step forward, and when Myles took a step back, he tripped over a tree root and fell to the ground. As Uncle Skeeta moved closer, Myles filled his hands with loose dirt. One more move from Uncle Skeeta, and Myles would throw the dirt in his face and run as fast as he could.

But just as Myles was about to take action, he noticed something on Uncle Skeeta's face. It was the smallest of smiles, but it was just enough to inspire Myles to delay his attack. A second later, the smile grew, and then Uncle

Skeeta started to laugh, softly at first, but then it became a full belly laugh. That's what happens when you realize that your mind just might be playing tricks on you—making you believe that a young boy, who clearly got lost after a simple walk in the woods, might actually be a secret spy who is out to get you and all that you care about.

The very thought of it only made Uncle Skeeta laugh harder, and he finally took two more steps toward Myles and stuck out his hand. Myles grabbed it, and Uncle Skeeta helped him to his feet.

"You're not a spy, are you?" Uncle Skeeta joked, still holding Myles' hand.

Myles forced a smile and faked a laugh. "Oh yeah, I'm a total spy," he joked, opening his other hand. "And this dirt here is actually magic truth powder so I can get all your secrets."

Now they were both laughing. "That's what I thought," said Uncle Skeeta, playing along. "Sorry about that. I hope I didn't scare you. I guess I've been under a little stress lately."

"No harm done. It was actually kind of fun," said Myles. He wiped his hand on his jeans and stuck it out for Uncle Skeeta to shake. "I'll just be on my way."

"Nonsense," replied Uncle Skeeta. "What type of person would I be if I left you alone? Do you even know what you've stumbled into?"

Myles shook his head.

"Well, it's something pretty amazing," said Uncle Skeeta. "But that can wait. You must be hungry. I'm making my famous campfire nachos. Why don't you join us? And then we'll figure out what to do with you."

Myles shook his head again, but this time he shook it adamantly, meaning eating with the Scallywaggers was definitely not part of the plan. He recited every excuse he could think of to respectfully decline the invitation. "I'm not hungry. I'm horrible company. I'm nacho intolerant. I had two dinners yesterday. I'm on a hunger strike."

But no matter what he tried, Uncle Skeeta just smiled and responded with, "I insist," and the next thing Myles knew, he was sitting at a campfire, eating nachos with the very people he had promised to defeat.

Crummy Tea

Grammy was as happy as a sloth as she sank deep into her rainbow beanbag chair and even deeper into the Spanish version of one of her favorite mystery novels. This was her time to be alone, a time she cherished because it was when she was most connected to the universe.

Of course, Grammy understood that this time to herself would be interrupted at some point soon, so she wasn't the least bit surprised when the front door of her cottage flew open with a force and fury that shook the windows and rattled the walls. After all, if a girl desperately seeking adventure runs away to your home, it's not unreasonable that her protective grandmother would be there soon enough. Especially when you intentionally posted a picture on Instagrammy so La Tarántula would know just where to find you.

"Oh, I'm so glad you're here," smiled Grammy, holding up her mystery novel. "I'm at a critical part of my book, and I can't figure out the meaning of 'El panadero sólo fingía estar muerto.'"

"I have come for my granddaughter," snapped La Tarántula from the doorway.

"Really?" responded Grammy, rereading the excerpt from the book. "That's quite a plot twist. There isn't even a granddaughter in the book."

La Tarántula grew angrier. "This is not about your book," she yelled in a loud, threatening tone. "This is about my granddaughter. Give me her location this instant."

"I have no idea where she is at this instant," replied Grammy. "It's been a long trip, I imagine. Please sit down, and we can share some tea." Before La Tarántula knew what was happening, Grammy escorted her to the living room and then headed to the kitchen for treats. A few minutes later, she returned with two cups of her favorite turmeric and cinnamon tea and a dozen stale ginger cookies.

"I don't want any crummy tea," replied La Tarántula, folding her arms.

"Don't worry, my tea is never crummy," said Grammy, placing the teacup on the table in front of the couch. "That's why I use stale cookies, so when you dip them into the tea, they don't fall apart."

Grammy demonstrated by dipping a cookie and then taking a sip of the tea. "Ahhh," she said. "Tea and stale cookies are the perfect prescription for whatever ails you."

Grammy's tone was peaceful and friendly, the exact opposite of her guest's, which made perfect sense, because although both women were grandmothers, that might have been the only thing they had in common.

"Let me get this straight," snapped La Tarántula, with more steam coming from her temper than from the teacup. "While my granddaughter is out there somewhere, you think it's smart for you to just sit in here, by yourself, doing nothing."

"Oh, I'm not doing nothing," said Grammy. "I'm being alone. There's something about being alone that I truly love. My grandmother's sister, Minny, was the same way." Grammy lifted her book right up to her nose. "Now if I can just figure out the meaning of El panadero sólo fingía estar muerto.'"

"You have no idea who you're dealing with," yelled La Tarántula.

"Really?" responded Grammy, rereading the excerpt from the book. "They don't usually threaten like that in this story. Interesting twist."

La Tarántula sprang to her feet and waved her arms as she barked, bellowed, and threatened some more. As always, Grammy stayed calm, and it didn't take much longer before La Tarántula realized that she could not bully Grammy the way she bullied other people in her life.

The truth was that Grammy was a comforting force, and, after a lot more silence and a little more talk, La Tarántula realized that she actually felt more at ease by just being in Grammy's house. There was something soothing about the soft candles, stacks of books, and a unique collection of potpourri, which is a mixture of dried flower petals and spices that Grammy created because she believed the auras were better for her than regular exercise.

Finally, the silence turned to honest and open

conversation, which is the best way for two sides that seem so different to finally understand that *different* can, and should, be good. La Tarántula listened as Grammy offered her feelings on magic and imagination and how every experience can be a good one with a little perspective. And Grammy listened as La Tarántula countered with her visions of danger and loss and how children need to be protected, no matter what.

"I failed at that job once. And I'm not doing it again," said La Tarántula. She paused for a second, a little embarrassed and a little relieved about sharing such a personal feeling. It was the first step in a healing process that was long overdue.

"You see, I used to be like you," added La Tarántula. "I used to see only the good in people. But when bad things happen to people you love, your spirit tends to shift to a much darker place. Then you start doing things that you're sure seem right at the time even if you know deep down inside that they're not." La Tarántula paused and thought about Rosalina.

"Do you know that I don't even let Rosalina sit on her own balcony after dark?" admitted La Tarántula as she slumped back, hoping the couch would swallow her alive. "She loves the stars, and I won't even let her see them. It got so bad that she invented an imaginary friend, a big brother, who she believed would always keep her safe."

Grammy thought of what to say next and decided not to say anything. Instead, she offered La Tarántula another stale cookie and a warm hug. La Tarántula accepted them both. After a few moments of a peaceful silence and one more cup of tea, La Tarántula finally took a deep breath, pointed to Grammy's book, and translated, "The baker was only pretending to be dead."

"I knew it," said Grammy, springing from the couch. She grabbed another stale cookie and offered it to La Tarántula. "You can never trust the baker."

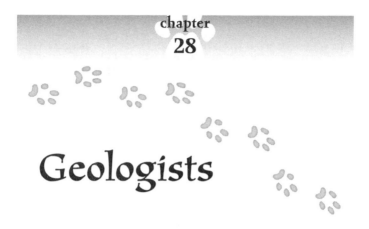

Geologists

Rudy's eyes grew wide, and he started jumping around after only a few bites of the nachos.

"Hot, hot, hot," he yelled, waving his hand over his mouth. He grabbed a canteen of water and desperately chugged as much and as fast as his mouth and belly would allow.

"A little spicier than normal, I guess," said Uncle Skeeta, who actually enjoyed the extra spark. "Keep eating," he said to Rudy before switching his gaze to Myles. "You too," he added. "You'll need your energy."

Myles nodded, and together he and Rudy finished all the nachos, consuming enough water to bathe a baby hippopotamus.

"This has been a good day," acknowledged Felonious.

He placed a roasted marshmallow on a graham cracker and relaxed by the fire with the other Scallywaggers, who were enjoying all the peace and possibilities that filled the night air. "Tomorrow will be an even better day."

"What's going on tomorrow?" asked Myles.

"We're getting the first piece of the Rock of Sarraka," blurted Rudy. Felonious and Uncle Skeeta glanced at each other. Secrets and pet squirrels: They're both tough to keep.

"Rock of Sarraka? Wow, that sounds pretty awesome," said Myles. "What are you guys, geologists?" Myles smiled. "I always wanted to be a geologist. You know, try to find the coolest rocks. So what's so special about this Rock of Sarraka?"

Felonious stared at Myles cautiously, then looked to Uncle Skeeta. They had already talked privately about Myles. At first, Felonious was suspicious. It was certainly odd to see another boy in Sarraka. But when Uncle Skeeta explained the details of Myles' story—where he was hiking, when he arrived—Felonious believed that Myles just might be telling the truth.

Still, Felonious paused and stared Myles up and down, from the bottom of his secondhand high-tops to the top of his tattered hooded sweatshirt, before finally admitting, "Yes, we're geologists." And he wasn't totally lying, because they were technically looking for rocks that held the secrets to the universe, which is exactly what geologists do.

He told Myles that they were highly trained experts who were sent to Sarraka to collect the three pieces of this very special rock. This fieldwork, as it was called by geologists, was dangerous and complicated.

"First, we need to find all three pieces to gain the full power of the rock," explained Felonious. "Second, the rock was split perfectly so if any of the three pieces are chipped or broken, the power of Sarraka is broken as well, and the world will crumble. And finally, once all three of the pieces are collected, the only place to reconnect them is back at the Pleasant Tree."

"What's a pleasant tree?" asked Myles.

"Oh, just something nice you say to start a conversation. Like 'Cool backpack,' or 'Nice weather we're having,' or 'It's nice to have another kid in Sarraka,'" answered Rudy with a warm smile.

After cleaning up the campsite, drinking some more water, and singing a few songs about rocks, volcanoes, and favorite foods that seem a little too spicy, Myles wished the Scallywaggers luck on their rock-finding mission, said good night, and started to walk away.

"Where are you going?" shouted Rudy. Before Myles could answer, he added, "Why don't you camp with us for the night? I mean, if you're lost, you shouldn't be wandering around on your own at night."

Again, Myles tried his best to refuse: "I snore like a wounded cow, I sleep tickle, I need some 'me' time." But the Scallywaggers could be pretty persistent, and, before he knew it, Uncle Skeeta had set up another tent right next to Rudy's.

A small part of Myles actually felt bad for what he was about to do. He had to admit, he was actually enjoying the Scallywaggers, even though he was pretty sure he shouldn't be. Rudy was different and clever in an interesting way. Felonious was super-smart and obviously cared deeply about Sarraka, and Myles wished everyone had an uncle as fun as Uncle Skeeta.

Still, he had a plan, and *There's too much at stake*, he told himself. So he went into his tent and made sure he didn't fall asleep.

Savage

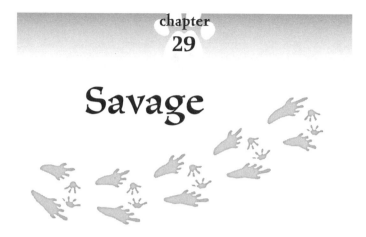

The thing about drinking a sea of water because you ate spicy nachos is that it can make you go to the bathroom in the middle of the night. So when Rudy left his tent after only a few hours of sleep, Myles flashed his devious smile and executed Step 5 of Operation Nachos: Poison Ivy on the Pillow.

Myles opened his bag of tricks and grabbed a pouch containing a three-leaf plant that is usually not welcome in campsites or anywhere else. Then, he snuck into Rudy's tent and rubbed a special, fast-acting type of poison ivy all over Rudy's pillow.

When the sun came up the next morning, Rudy couldn't see it. He couldn't see a thing, because his eyes were almost completely swollen shut, there was redness all over his cheeks, and his scalp was itching with fire and fury.

"What happened?" asked Felonious, as Rudy ran from the tent in misery.

"Ooh," added Uncle Skeeta, his face scrunching together as if he could almost feel Rudy's pain. "That doesn't look good."

"It doesn't feel good, either," snapped Rudy, walking in circles, scratching his head, and mumbling words that shouldn't be repeated.

"How did this happen?" said Felonious, trying to get closer, but not too close. "You were fine last night when you went into your tent."

Rudy paused for a second to think and then pointed in the direction of Myles' tent. "He did this," Rudy accused.

"What are you talking about?" said Uncle Skeeta. "Why? How?"

"Think about it," said Rudy, tapping the side of his head, which turned into scratching the side of his head.

"All of a sudden he shows up, the nachos are too spicy, I drink all that water, I go to the bathroom, and when I wake up the next morning," he pointed to his face, "I look like one of those Shar-pei dogs."

"Try not to scratch," advised Felonious. "It only makes it worse."

"That's the lamest advice I've ever heard," snapped Rudy. And he continued to scratch, which only made it worse.

Myles listened carefully from inside his tent as Felonious and Uncle Skeeta considered Rudy's accusation. They didn't want to believe it at first, but, after further discussion, they couldn't think of another logical explanation, except for sometimes when you camp, you get poison ivy.

Myles knew he would be a suspect. It's exactly why he didn't want to have dinner with the Scallywaggers, why he definitely didn't want to camp with them, and why, in the middle of the night, he knew he had to do the one thing that would make it obvious that it was not his fault.

"Ooh," said Uncle Skeeta as Myles appeared from his tent. Uncle Skeeta's face was scrunching in the same way it did minutes earlier when Rudy emerged in the same condition. "That doesn't look good."

"It doesn't feel good either," Myles grumbled, scratching his scalp, which only made it worse.

Myles turned toward Rudy. "Wow, it looks like we're both in this together," he said, forcing a grin, and all Rudy could do was feel just a little worse that he had accused his new friend of something so devious. After all, you'd have to be as sly as a swift fox to rub poison ivy all over someone else's pillow and then do the same thing to your own pillow, just to make it seem like you were innocent. And that's exactly what Myles did.

"I'm so sorry," said Rudy.

"For what?" replied Myles. "You didn't do this to me. It was probably just an honest mistake. Maybe I got it when I was going to the bathroom in the middle of the night. We did drink a lot of water."

Rudy agreed that there was probably a logical explanation. And together they moved into Uncle Skeeta's tent and lay down with their heads on pillows, waiting as patiently as could be expected while Felonious and Uncle Skeeta went in search of an aloe plant, which was nature's way of helping.

"Can I tell you something?" said Rudy, after a short silence. He picked up his head and looked around to make sure no one was listening. "Believe it or not, you're probably my only friend right now," Rudy admitted in a sad and serious tone. "And I didn't trust you."

"Don't sweat it," said Myles. "I'm not a very trustworthy guy. I once set all the clocks ahead five hours and then woke my sister up in the middle of the night and told her it was time to go to school."

"Savage," Rudy said, and even though it hurt to smile, it was still worth it.

"I don't have a sister or a brother," said Rudy. "Or not a real one. I used to have a best friend," he added. "We were like brothers."

"Used to?" repeated Myles. "What happened?"

There was a moment of silence, as Rudy considered exactly how much of the story to share. Then he decided to share it all. "He stabbed me in the back," said Rudy. "Turned on me for no reason, and now he's going out of his way to make my life miserable. What type of friend does that?" asked Rudy.

"Not a very good one," agreed Myles.

Rudy let out a deep sigh as if the weight of the world was finally starting to catch up. "What am I even doing here? My face is swollen shut, I'm lying in a tent spilling my guts to a kid I just met, and I'm supposed to be strong enough to track down one of the most powerful rocks in the universe. I don't think I can do it. I think I'm just an ordinary kid."

Myles squinted back at Rudy, shrugged, and replied simply, "There's no such thing."

Surf's Up, Dude

Maybe it was the cool, soothing ointment from the aloe plants, or maybe it was that he had a new friend to share the experience with, but either way, Rudy actually felt better.

During the next several days, the inspiration continued to grow, as the swelling in his face went down. With his eyesight struggling, the rest of his senses improved. He could smell the sweet fragrances all around him. He could hear the rhythms of the land in a way that he never could before.

It took almost eight days for Rudy's mind, body, and spirit to heal completely. On the ninth day, he rose with the sun to begin the journey to the volcano. It was only a three-hour hike, and this time, Myles didn't try to resist when he was invited to come along. He even helped Uncle Skeeta and Felonious lower Rudy into the huge, hollow rock with hot lava all around.

Finding your way in a large volcano is a challenge for even the most experienced geologist, and at first Rudy was confused, disoriented, even scared. He was protected from the heat by a white insulated suit, but when he flipped on the headlight, all the paths and tunnels and rocks seemed exactly the same.

He tried to call Felonious for help, but the heat from the lava melted the microphone on his radio. Rudy wiped his hands on his suit, and for a second considered shooting the flare into the air to signal that he was ready to be pulled back up. But then a calmness engulfed him like a warm blanket, and even though his eyes and ears now worked perfectly, he realized that he could maneuver around better by just trusting his instincts.

It took hours to explore the inside of the volcano, but it felt like minutes to Rudy, who was starting to focus on the challenge instead of the results. He went right when his instincts told him to go right and left when they steered him to the left. Up, down, over, around, back and forth, try and fail, and try again until he finally saw exactly what he was looking for.

There was no doubt. The first piece of the Rock of Sarraka was just as Felonious described—a dark, red, jagged element resting in a small crevasse, which is a deep, open crack high up on a volcano wall. What Felonious failed to mention was that between the ledge Rudy was currently standing on and the wall the Rock was currently hiding in was a giant pond of hot lava —or it could have been a small lake—but either way, it looked tough to cross.

Rudy studied his surroundings. He told himself that problems were meant to be solved. Rudy dipped his hand into the pond.

"Ow," he yelled, waving his hand as if he were putting out a fire. The suit would protect him from the heat, but he realized it wasn't nearly strong enough to withstand direct contact with a substance that can reach a temperature of more than 1,000 degrees Celsius. Rudy stared into the hot lava that was flowing freely like waves rushing into the shore—big powerful waves that gave Rudy an idea.

He grabbed one of the two small spears from his belt and started chipping away at a long, narrow section of the ledge on which he stood. After just a few minutes, the section of stone, which happened to be just about the same size and shape as the surfboard Rudy used on his family vacations, floated into the lava.

I must be crazy, Rudy thought to himself. Then he jumped on the stone, lay down on his belly and balanced until his makeshift surfboard caught the perfect wave of lava. When the time was just right, Rudy pushed up with his hands and then popped into a standing position, riding the wave all the way across the lava to solid ground on the other side.

Savage, Rudy thought to himself, as he looked around, wishing someone else, particularly Brody, was there to see. But that was just the beginning. Now it was time to scale the wall, and Rudy knew just how to do it.

This time he grabbed both spears from his belt and held one in each hand. He stuck the first spear into the side of the wall and hung on tight. When his grip was sure, he stuck the second spear into the wall and pulled himself a little higher. He took a deep breath and looked up. He estimated that there were about twenty feet to go.

Brody can do this, he thought to himself. *And if Brody can do this, so can I*, which was just the Brodivation he needed.

With the second blade secured in his left hand, he removed the first one with his right hand, reached up, and stuck it into the wall, pulling himself even higher into the air. He continued this pattern, over and over, like he was climbing a ladder with just his arms, as his legs dangled below.

If Rudy's arms were getting tired, he quickly forgot it the instant he grabbed the first piece of the Rock of Sarraka—a red rock so pure that it seemed that it was nothing more than a ball full of fire. He could feel the power surge through his veins, and it made everything feel better.

"Be extra careful," Rudy told himself, repeating the warning from Felonious. Once separated, these rocks were as fragile as eggs, and if they suffered even the slightest scratch, nick, or break, Sarraka could be destroyed.

But Rudy had everything under control. He gently placed the rock into an insulated bag Uncle Skeeta had created just for this occasion. He didn't even need the flare. He easily retraced his steps to the entrance of the volcano and emerged with a proud grin, a powerful rock, and, most importantly to Rudy, one-third of Brody Boondoggle's powers.

chapter
31

Rock

Brody's grip started to weaken, and he lost his concentration at the worst possible time. But that's what happens when your spirit feels like a basketball that won't bounce because a third of the air is leaking out.

He was traveling through a long, underground tube or pipeline, kind of like a sewer. It was dark and stinky, but it was the final stretch on the way to the Baffling Brook, the only place in the region where a portion of the water mysteriously stops flowing.

Few people, if any, ever saw the Baffling Brook for themselves. Why risk a trip through a 500-foot tube that was almost completely filled with water? Oh, there were a few inches of air on the top, but to make it through successfully, you had to travel on your back, keeping your nose and mouth as high as possible so you could breathe. One slip and you better grow gills or be a crab, because you were going to have to take your next breath under water.

"Toughen up," Jake yelled, as he reached down with one hand and pulled Brody back up by the scruff of his T-shirt. "You have to focus."

"It's not that easy," Brody replied, gasping for air. "I'm dealing with a lot of stuff here that you clearly don't understand."

"I understand you need to toughen up," replied Jake, and while they moved one hand over the other, the two brothers continued to say things to each other that they would never say to anyone else.

A few insults later, they finally made it through the pipe where the rest of SWEEPE was waiting. The hot sun was already drying their clothes, but it was also taking its toll, particularly on Brody, who crawled into the shade of a nearby tree.

Punching Crab recognized the look on Brody's face. Brody seemed tired and worn out, so Punching Crab crawled over to join him. "Tell me what you see?" whispered Punching Crab, trying to keep Brody focused. "What's going on in Sarraka?"

Brody took a deep breath and considered the questions. "It's hard to tell," he said, staring in the distance with his right, pink eye. "I see images, but they're starting to get blurry."

Punch considered everything he knew about Sarraka and the power of the Akaway. Then he scurried up to Brody's shoulder and stared into his eyes.

"What is it?" Brody asked, anxiously.

"Your eye. It's losing its pink," said Punch. "That means they must have captured the first piece of the rock." Brody dropped his head and closed his eyes. "Don't worry," added Punch. "It's only a third, so you're still connected. You're just not as strong."

"Tell me something I don't know," said Brody with a sigh.

"A billy goat pees on its own head to smell more attractive for females," shrugged Punch. He thought for a second and added, "And a hug is scientifically proven to make you feel better." He gave Brody a big, healing hug.

"The point is, it's not over yet," said Punch. "As long as there is some pink left in your eye, it means we have hope. And when you have hope, anything is possible." Then he handed Brody the "Gone for Good Wart Cream" he had stolen from Brody's back pocket during the hug.

"I'm trying to quit," Punching Crab promised.

Brody sighed and secretly admitted that the hug did help. After all, he might not be at his best, but he was still on a mission that was important and tough in all the right ways. So he took five deep breaths, stood up, and joined the rest of SWEEPE just as Alec was explaining what made this particular brook so baffling.

"This part flows to the south, and this part flows to the north," said Alec, pointing in different directions. "And this part in the middle doesn't flow at all. I've heard that some people consider it to be the absolute center of the universe."

Rosalina opened the binder that belonged to Felonious and grabbed the other two pages Jake had identified as different but good. After careful review, she focused on the page that was hard and grainy like a thin slate of rock. Rosalina flipped it over and noticed that the slate was blank on both sides, which really wasn't much help. Then she remembered the Baffling Brook.

"It's all connected."

Rosalina dipped the rocky slate into the water that flowed south. Nothing. She dipped it into the water that flowed north. Still nothing. Then she dipped the slate into the water that wasn't flowing at all, and it revealed just what they needed: a hidden message.

"The *WORLD*," read Alec, noticing that the *W* and *O* in world were both darker than the rest of the letters. Under the words was an actual map of the world. Ten countries were also darker. On the bottom of the page were four short lines, then a space, two more short lines, then another space, and six more lines. Twelve lines, ten countries.

"Rwanda, Turkey, Libya, France, Australia, Hungary, Spain, Lesotho, Oman, Norway," said Alec, identifying the countries like the geography champ that he was. As he announced each country, Rosalina wrote down the first letter in the sand: *R, T, L, F, A, H, S, L, O, N*. Then she added *W* and *O* from *world*.

"*Wort Ha Lofsln,*" yelled Punch, seconds after SWEEPE formed a circle around the letters.

"No, no," Punch corrected. "How about *Trof So Lawnlh? Slow Ho Tranlf? Flat On Wrohls?* Wait a second. I almost have it. *Horn At Wollfs.*"

After a few more suggestions that didn't make much more sense, Brody and Jake finally realized that the first word probably started with a *W*, because that was the first letter of *world.* After mixing around the letters, Jake suggested *wall,* and when he heard that, Brody guessed the second word was *of.*

"*Wall of . . .*" Rosalina started, and before she could finish, Alec blurted out, "*thorns.* Let's go."

Scissors

The journey to find the Wall of Thorns was intense from the start, which was great for Rosalina, whose spirit soared as SWEEPE worked together to forge paths, climb peaks, and cross bridges, and not so good for Brody, who tried to stay positive even as his spirit was moving in the opposite direction, continually getting weaker, if only by a third.

They talked very little except to say things like, "This might be the hottest day of the year," or "The Wall of Thorns is just around the next bend," or "When I was a kid, I wanted to be a boat."

A short break for Grammy's homemade taco salad wraps, chocolate chip granola bars, and bacon-flavored popcorn provided just the burst of energy SWEEPE needed to fuel their bodies. And the final piece of the different but good material in the binder was just what they needed to inspire their minds.

When they arrived at the massive Wall of Thorns, Rosalina unfolded the extra-large piece of paper three times before it reached its full size. There was a single word—*violet*—written on one side of the paper and dash marks along the edges. But as hard as they tried, SWEEPE couldn't imagine how this "different" piece of paper would help.

"What kind of scam is this?" griped Alec, before convincing himself that a little thorn could never stop a rough and tough badger. Of course, these thorns were not little, and even though he touched them only gently, he still jumped when his finger was pricked.

"Ow," yelled the rough and tough badger. "Stupid thorns."

The ocelot in Jake didn't have any better luck using his agility to scale the wall, and the armadillo in Rosalina couldn't break through the thorns, which was odd because that's what an armadillo's armor is for. But this was no ordinary wall. It was one of the last lines of defense for the Grappling Mountains, the entryway into Sarraka. So even though Brody tried to match the Wall of Thorns by focusing on a thorny dragon, it was obvious that all those protective spines covering the Australian lizard were still not nearly strong enough, especially when Brody wasn't at full strength.

"Let's figure this out," said Rosalina, opening a notebook from her Hoodster. "The rock was just what we needed at the brook." She wrote down the word *rock*. "The piece of paper really helped with the book." She scribbled the word *paper*. "What could we possibly use to get through these thorns?"

She looked down at her notes and read, "Rock, paper," and just like that, everyone yelled, "Scissors," except for Punch, who yelled, "Monkey."

"That's what we need to break through," announced Rosalina.

Of course, no Hoodster would be complete without a super-strong pair of scissors. Rosalina handed Jake the paper from the binder, grabbed the scissors, and immediately tried cutting through the thorns. But even these scissors weren't strong enough to impact the thorns. As Jake watched Rosalina unsuccessfully cut, slice, and stab, he realized he was still holding the oversized piece of paper. It had to have a purpose.

"It kind of looks like a small door," said Jake, holding it out at arm's length.

"Almost like a doggie door," added Alec.

"Or a monkey door," said Punch.

And since it couldn't hurt to try, Jake walked up to the thorns and leaned the paper at the bottom of the wall as if it were the perfect way through. But the flimsy paper simply fell to the ground, and each time Jake picked it up and tried again, the wall seemed to stubbornly grow taller and thicker.

"That's not good," said Rosalina, her neck bending further and further back.

"What about the violet? Maybe that's a clue," Brody wondered. "Maybe the wall is color-coded."

"If it is, the colors are either inside the wall or on the other side," said Alec. "How can we identify the right color if we can't see it?"

Punching Crab raised his claw and started jumping

around. "I can smell colors," he promised. That claim caused a bunch of eye rolls and sarcastic comments, but, in the end, SWEEPE agreed that Punching Crab and his ability to smell colors just might be their last hope.

Punch paced back and forth with his nose as close to the wall as possible. "Why did it have to be violet?" he moaned. "I can smell blue a mile away. And yellow is a piece of cake. Laga, laga, laga."

Punching Crab was freaking out under the pressure, so Jake pulled him aside and said the perfect thing to convince Punch that this was his moment, and that if he could truly smell colors, then he could smell all colors, including violet. Punch nodded and took a deep breath while Alec put his head in his hands. "How can we be this desperate?"

But Punch was gaining confidence with each sniff. And he finally stopped in front of one section of the wall and pointed. "This is violet," he said. "I can smell it."

Everyone watched as Jake grabbed the paper and walked to where Punch was pointing. He placed the paper at the base of the wall, and this time, the flimsy paper didn't fall to the ground. Instead, it stuck perfectly to the violet section of the Wall of Thorns that only Punching Crab could smell.

"Yes," whispered Punching Crab to himself as he pumped his claw.

"I knew you could do it," bragged Alec.

"Try cutting along the dashes," Jake suggested to Rosalina, and when she did, the scissors easily sliced through the thorns as if they were nothing more than a wall of whipped cream or butterscotch pudding.

"Three challenges up and three challenges down," said Brody, as he pushed the door open with his feet so everyone could climb through. "It should be smooth sailing now."

Team SWEEPE took a few minutes to breathe, stretch, drink, and do anything else to relax, because they wanted to believe that Brody was right. That there would be no more trouble on their way to the Grappling Mountains, that they were dangerously close to finally getting into Sarraka, and that there was no need to be worried that the grizzly bear off in the distance was heading their way.

Falkland Island Wolf

Alec took off like a badger chasing a chicken. Rosalina was close behind, running in a zigzag pattern because she had learned by playing with Myles that animals with four legs, like rabbits, swift foxes, and grizzly bears, cannot turn as quickly as animals with two legs.

It took a little longer, but Brody eventually thought of a red kangaroo, the perfect animal, because the faster it hops, the less energy it uses, and Brody didn't have energy to spare. Jake threw the last of the equipment into his own backpack and then bolted as well.

"Fun fact," yelled Alec from the front of the pack. "When you're running from a bear with a group of people, you don't actually have to outrun the bear. You only have to outrun the slowest person in your group."

"That is a fun fact," said Punch, cruising through the sand as fast as his crab legs would take him. He looked back quickly to see that the only creature behind him was the bear. "Hey," he yelled. "We're all in this together, right?"

Just as the bear was about to move into striking distance, Jake slowed down enough to scoop Punch up and put him on his shoulders.

"Right," said Jake.

The bear growled when Jake darted to the left with the quickness of an ocelot.

Even as Brody was running, he couldn't help thinking that something didn't make sense. Bears are normally reclusive animals, meaning they like to be by themselves. But this bear clearly had SWEEPE on its mind.

Brody glanced at Punch, who acknowledged that even with just one-third of Brody's powers, Rudy was easily strong enough to talk with the animals and even control them. They figured out that this bear was here to slow SWEEPE down, or maybe worse.

At first, Brody refused to believe that Rudy could do such a thing. Maybe it was a miscommunication with the grizzly. But when Brody concentrated, focusing all his energies on the bear, which was moving toward them with an unmistakable purpose, Brody immediately knew Punching Crab was right. "That bear is not himself right now, and he won't listen to me," said Brody, who grew more tired from the interaction.

Brody's eyes widened when he looked into the distance and saw a mountain. *If we can just get there*, he thought, *we might have a chance.* Brody glanced at the bear, then ahead at the mountain. Then again and again, each time calculating and recalculating the distance they needed to travel compared with the speed at which the bear was moving. But the math didn't work. The bear was closing in, and the mountain was too far away.

Brody dug deeper, trying to find the energy to run faster, and encouraged the rest of SWEEPE to do the same. Instead, Brody found something else. His right eye wasn't completely pink like it should be, but there was still a connection, and when he looked up with that eye, he saw something off in the distance.

At first, he thought it was just a dog, but a few moments later, he realized he was looking at a very special creature known as the Falkland Island wolf, which was known for its kind and gentle spirit. Unfortunately, it was that playful nature that had led to its extinction, because the wolf was easily hunted for its valuable fur. But a little thing like being extinct couldn't stop the power of Sarraka.

The Falkland Island wolf started slowly, and then it gained speed as it cruised past Alec, around Rosalina, and through Jake's legs toward the grizzly. The bear seemed shocked at first, and then it seemed annoyed as it slowed down and swatted the wolf with its enormous but quick paws. The wolf pranced and danced and dodged the punches. He nipped at the bear's legs and then darted away, a routine that was obviously causing the bear frustration and distracting him at the same time.

When the bear looked one way, the wolf quickly darted the other way, ran up the bear's leg, and stopped right between its shoulder blades. The bear bucked, and, for just a moment, it seemed like the two animals were actually enjoying each other—the wolf pretending to be a cowboy and the bear pretending to be a bucking bronco.

Finally, the bear rolled over on its back, which is when the wolf jumped off and skipped away in the shadows.

"Thank you," whispered Brody, and the Falkland Island wolf howled to say, "We're all rooting for you."

By the time the bear was back in pursuit, SWEEPE had reached the base of the mountain. Brody started scaling the terrain as easily as a bighorn sheep, or at least a weaker bighorn sheep, and motioned for everyone to follow behind, which probably wasn't necessary because when there's a bear closing in, you tend to try to keep moving as fast as possible.

The group finally stopped on a narrow ledge about one hundred feet off the ground. Brody scooted over, and everyone else sat down. "Bears can climb, but I don't think he will. He'll probably give up and leave us alone," predicted Brody, who was only half right. The bear didn't try to climb the mountain, but he didn't leave either. And when the sun finally set and lit up the sky in all the right ways, the bear simply lay down, shifted slightly to get a little more comfortable, and fell asleep.

chapter
34

Operation Flying Time

No matter how hard Myles plotted or schemed, he just couldn't find a way to slow down time. The first piece of the rock was safely sealed in a hyperbaric air chamber, meaning it was perfectly protected at all times. Now, after several days of hiking and biking and controlling animals, the Rock Tracker was leading the Scallywaggers and Myles directly to the second piece of the Rock of Sarraka.

"You must be our good luck charm," Felonious said to Myles as they followed the Rock Tracker to the end of a long, narrow pier. One by one, they climbed into a wooden boat that rested on a body of water that could have been a sea, a gulf, a lake, or something completely different. It didn't really matter, because, just like everything else in Sarraka, it was perfect.

Even Myles couldn't stop himself from enjoying the ride. Sure, this was an important part of his adventure that he never expected, but he was still in Sarraka, and it was almost impossible not to enjoy. As they floated over the rapids, Myles realized that maybe he had been thinking about this all wrong. Instead of trying to slow time down, it would be better to make it fly.

Myles didn't know about storifly, but that was okay. It didn't take him long to come up with a plan he called Operation Flying Time.

Step 1. *Think of a list of ways to have fun, which everyone knows is another great way to make time fly.*

"Last one in is a rotten bumbershoot," challenged Myles, and he dove right off the boat. Uncle Skeeka had no idea that a bumbershoot was actually an umbrella, but he knew he didn't want to be a rotten one, so he dove in as well. The truth was, Uncle Skeeta was clearly affected by the power of Sarraka, and he just wanted to have fun.

"They have to be kidding," sighed Rudy, who was

completely focused on collecting the second piece of the rock. But Felonious just put up his fin to say, "Let it go, there's nothing you can do."

Step 2. Let the games begin.

Without wasting a second, Myles used his spirit-animal skills to talk to a giant spider crab, a goblin shark, and a dragonfish, and, just like that, they had enough creatures for a marathon game of hide-and-seek.

Of course, when you have a super-long snout that allows you to detect even the tiniest electrical currents given off by all living things, the game isn't exactly fair. So, the goblin shark had to agree not to use its nose if the dragonfish agreed not to use its ability to produce light. The spider crab didn't have to agree to anything, but it still lost every game—sometimes it's hard being the largest crab in the world.

Hide-and-seek morphed into a game of cops-and-robbers when Myles convinced a vampire squid, a big red jellyfish, and a gulper eel that joining the fun would do a world of good for Sarraka. There was plenty of room for Rudy to join, but fun wasn't his motivation—collecting rocks was—so he declined at first, choosing instead to join

Felonious on a nearby sandbar where they continued to practice the spirit-animal skills that Rudy now possessed.

Step 3. Remember, fun doesn't have to end.

Minutes turned to hours and hours turned to days as Myles's creativity soared, and he found more ways to make fun happen. After a fantastic finish in a game called Chest Ball that they invented, Myles introduced Uncle Skeeta to a megamouth shark, a viperfish, and a fangtooth, and the next thing they knew, a week had passed while they started their own band called Doozy Paloozy; wrote a few songs, like "Brownies for Breakfast" and "Hobo with an Oboe"; and played their first gig for a school of guppies. Uncle Skeeta wished Gizmo was there, because he could really jam on the bass guitar.

And while the band was a total hit, even without Gizmo, not everyone believed it was the best use of time.

"What happened to you?" barked Rudy when Uncle Skeeta finally returned from his tour. "You know we're racing the clock here."

"Actually, he's not wasting time at all," corrected Felonious. He pulled the vitality meter from his belt, flipped it open, and showed it to Rudy. The needle that had been moving slowly to the red was now actually moving slightly to the green. "He's been having fun. And in Sarraka, fun equals energy," explained Felonious. "So if you want to create extra time in Sarraka, it's simple. Just have fun."

Rudy furrowed his eyebrows and shook his head. "I'll remember that if I ever need to create more time," he said. "But right now what we need is to find the second rock before Brody gets here to stop us." He turned to Uncle Skeeta. "And we can't do that when you're off hanging out with every creature in the sea."

Uncle Skeeta just nodded his head and grinned. "Are you saying I'm being shellfish?" he said, as he and Myles climbed on the boat, grabbed the oars, and started rowing. A large scowl emerged on Rudy's face, which Uncle Skeeta immediately took as a challenge, and added, "Because I don't see why you're harping on me."

Rudy sighed in disgust. "I get it, I get it," he said, motioning for Uncle Skeeta to row a little faster. "Harp is a kind of fish—very funny. I'm just saying, why did you have to start a band?"

"Oh, I don't know," replied Uncle Skeeta, his eyebrows

scrunching down as he tried to imitate the scowl on Rudy's face. "I think I just did it for the halibut. If you want me to quit, just let minnow."

Myles was trying his hardest not to laugh, and Felonious couldn't help but giggle as he continued to follow the beeps of the Rock Tracker through a coral reef. The signal from the rock and the energy throughout Sarraka was even stronger, which is exactly what happens when fun is in the air.

"But we should dolphinately talk about how you're feeling," Uncle Skeeta continued, skillfully tickling Rudy's ribs with one of the oars. "Did you catch that one?" Uncle Skeeta added, raising his bushy eyebrows. "Because I've been dying to trout that joke for a while."

The corners of Rudy's mouth rose just a little as the easygoing part of Uncle Skeeta's personality brought him back to a time when Rudy and his uncle would just sit around, make jokes, and eat peanut butter and fluff sandwiches.

The memory made Rudy pause for a moment. He looked at Myles, who shrugged as if to say, "If you can't beat him. . . ." Then a scowl reappeared on Rudy's face.

He looked Uncle Skeeta in the eye and said, "Maybe it's time you stopped squidding around."

Tanks a Lot

Uncle Skeeta inserted his index finger into his right ear and wiggled it around to make sure he heard Rudy correctly. So did Myles. Rudy looked at them both and confirmed with a smirk, "Yes, I did that on porpoise." It was a great smirk, which is almost always better than a scowl, and Uncle Skeeta realized he hadn't seen one from Rudy in way too long.

"Now you're just fishing for compliments," replied Uncle Skeeta, and before they knew it, time was flying, as Uncle Skeeta and Rudy threw puns around like a baseball, back and forth, laughing and singing, and making up songs together like they did before little things like greed and revenge got in the way.

"You're all giving me a haddock," laughed Felonious, but then suddenly his laughter stopped, and the smile on his face was replaced by a look of panic, fear, or maybe both.

It was that feeling again, only this time it was worse. It was a vision of nothingness that caused Felonious to lose his balance and fall out of the boat. Uncle Skeeta quickly dove in after him.

"What is it?" asked Uncle Skeeta, floating next to Felonious. "Is there something you're not telling us?"

Felonious thought for a moment, but he didn't know what to say even if he wanted to. How do you describe a feeling that there is something out there that wants what you want, only worse? So instead, he composed himself by taking deep breaths and waited for the Rock Tracker to do its job.

"Look," Felonious said, pointing over the horizon. And when Rudy, Myles, and Uncle Skeeta raised their heads, they dropped their jaws, which is usually the first thing you do when you see maybe the most magnificent sight of your life in the not-so-far-off distance.

"Water," said Rudy, remembering the element that was

represented by the second piece of the Rock of Sarraka, and the giant spinning circles in the water indicated that this was the destination they were looking for. Now they just had to find the rock, and Rudy already knew how to do it.

Most scuba divers wear their equipment when they leave the boat, but that's not how it works when you're chasing the second piece of the Rock of Sarraka. Instead, Rudy gave Myles a fist pump and took five deep breaths, filling his lungs with as much oxygen as possible before diving deep into the water like a giant devil ray, which can dive down faster than almost any other fish.

Rudy kept his mind clear and his heart calm as he swam deeper and deeper down an underwater channel that was too small to fit both him and the equipment he would eventually need. It wasn't until he finally squeezed through a hole about the size of a large pizza that Felonious and Uncle Skeeta lowered the appropriate gear, including a mask, flippers, underwater map, and lights.

"Where are the air tanks?" asked Rudy through the intercom in the mask.

"Can you repeat that?" asked Uncle Skeeta.

"The air tanks I need to breathe," replied Rudy. "Shouldn't they be here?"

"The 'air' what?" said Uncle Skeeta.

"Tanks," yelled Rudy. "Tanks, tanks."

"You're welcome," said a grinning Uncle Skeeta, just as he lowered two yellow tanks down next to the rest of the equipment.

Rudy shook his head with a matching grin as he hooked up the first tank. He put on his flippers and adjusted his mask, and when he did, the grin turned into a genuine smile. It was like he was swimming in a giant aquarium, at one with thousands of exotic and unusual fish, sharks, turtles, and more, and Rudy took just a little extra time to appreciate the moment.

Finally, he spotted the underwater cave that matched the one on the map. Rudy inhaled one more time and headed into the dark chamber, filled with strong currents, narrow tunnels, and patches of underwater fog that were there to make divers so distracted and disoriented that they would panic and give up, or worse.

Rudy didn't appear again for more than two hours, because that's how long it took to master the underwater maze, enter the barracuda tornado, where hundreds of snakelike fish with sharp teeth swam around and around, and capture a blue rock so pure that it seemed it was nothing more than an oddly-shaped ball full of water. Rudy felt even more of Brody's power surge through his veins as he carefully placed the jagged rock into a protective container to make sure it wouldn't be chipped or broken.

"It's o-fish-al," beamed Rudy as he came back to the surface. "Two down, one to go."

Top of the World

The first sign read, *Nobody beyond this point*, but that didn't stop Rosalina. When you've spent almost your entire life being told to be careful and cautious, and you finally have a chance to do just the opposite, you're certainly not going to let a wooden sign stand in your way. Especially when you've just slept on a ledge for an entire night waiting for a grizzly bear to wake up, shake its head as if it had a terrible headache, and wander away, turning back only once to tell you that the mountains he had chased you to just might be the exact mountains you were looking for all along.

The next sign read, *Danger ahead, turn back at once*, which was probably good advice for most climbers, but Rosalina was not most climbers. She was an explorer, just like her brother, and right now she was hiking the unknown path up the Grappling Mountains that until now had only lived on her wall and in her brother's dreams.

The final sign read, *If you've come this far, you're clearly not listening anyway, so just do whatever you want*. And that's exactly what Rosalina did, going higher and higher with a combination of courage and drive that can only come from being free for the first time.

The rest of SWEEPE tipped their heads back as they watched Rosalina slide across a narrow opening that led to the back of the mountain. She was out of sight for what seemed like a little too long, but nobody was worried or even surprised when she re-emerged on the other side. Rosalina put her hands in the air and yelled as loud as possible, because, at that moment, she was truly on top of the world.

"She did it," admired Alec, who was too inspired to stay still. He grabbed his backpack and darted up the same path. Jake and Punch followed closely behind until they realized Brody wasn't coming.

Of course, Jake didn't care that Brody's spirit was draining again. He didn't notice that Brody's right eye had now lost two-thirds of its pink and that he only had one-third of his power left. Climbing up such a difficult trail was like riding a three-wheeled bike up a giant hill with two flat tires.

"Toughen up," barked Jake as he traversed back down the mountain. Brody wanted to respond with some kind of comeback that included the words *ugly boy*, but he was too tired. So instead, he put his arm around Jake's shoulder, and they climbed to the top of the hill together.

"Strange," said Rosalina, who was scanning the area in all directions. "There's nothing here. It's like the trail just vanished."

Brody poured a bottle of water over his head. *You have to be kidding me*, he thought to himself. While everyone split up to search for a way to cross the cavern, Brody took five deep breaths, picked himself up, and followed his instincts down one path and then another. But in the end, Rosalina was right. The bridge over the massive gully that was in the picture on Rosalina's wall was nowhere to be seen.

Brody was drained and confused. His powers were getting weaker, and it seemed the harder he tried to connect, the less connected he actually became.

"Are you okay?" asked Rosalina, who had secretly followed Brody. She put her hand on Brody's shoulder.

"I can't do it," said Brody, staring into the distance. "I know there's something out there to help us, but I can't find it." He took one more deep, depressing sigh and crumbled to the ground. "I just feel like an ordinary kid."

Rosalina yanked Brody's shoulder, which forced their eyes to connect. "There's no such thing," she said with a smile.

When Brody gazed into Rosalina's deep blue eyes, he saw such confidence and hope that he couldn't help but smile back. He grabbed Rosalina's hand, and when he did, Brody could feel a new wave of energy surge through his spirit. He still wasn't at his strongest, but with Rosalina's help, he was strong enough to keep trying.

Brody took five more deep breaths, in through his nose and out through his mouth, and listened with his heart to the auras of the land. That's when he heard maybe the most beautiful sound in the universe: laughter. Brody sprang to his feet and followed the laughter to the edge of the cliff. But again, there was nothing there—no trees, no signs, no anything—just emptiness and a laugh.

"You're here," he whispered. "I can feel it."

In that instant, the hint of pink that was left in his right eye started to focus. Suddenly, the laughter stopped, and a beautiful bird with light brown feathers and yellowish-brown stripes appeared for the first time in a hundred years.

"A laughing owl," Brody affirmed, and the owl laughed a shrieking cry that basically meant, "It's good to see you, too." The owl laughed a little more before gracefully flying along the edge of the cliff, finally stopping about thirty feet away. Brody nodded because it made perfect sense.

"This is where we cross," he said, and the owl laughed again to let Brody know that he was right. "Thank you," Brody whispered, and the owl flew away with the pride that comes from knowing you did your part.

"That was the coolest thing I've ever seen," whispered Rosalina.

"You saw that?" Brody whispered back.

"I guess I did," Rosalina admitted. "I saw that wolf, too," she confessed, before adding that she was very young when she first started seeing animals that most people thought were imaginary. "I never said anything, because I was scared, but when El Pantsing Crab mentioned it in the prison, everything made sense." She looked at Brody. "Do you think I'm crazy?"

Brody shook his head. "We're all a little crazy," he said with a warm smile that led to an awkward silence. It lasted only a few seconds before Jake, Alec, and Punch rushed over, and suddenly the moment was gone, and it was back to the mission.

Brody walked to the exact spot the laughing owl indicated, and peered over the side of the cliff. He saw nothing. Well, maybe not nothing. There was a cloud. Well, not just any cloud. It was a soft, fluffy, white cloud with just a hint of pink around the edges. At first, this particular cloud seemed out of place, floating alone in the middle of an all-blue sky. But then Brody heard a voice deep in his spirit, *trust your instincts*, and suddenly this cloud felt perfectly right.

Brody closed his left eye and stared at the cloud with his right eye, the eye that was getting weaker but was still desperately hanging on to the hint of pink around the edges. In that moment, Brody could swear he felt the lone cloud with the same hint of pink staring back at him, studying his auras, filling his spirit in ways that can only happen when you have a lifelong friendship with nature.

When the time felt right, Brody opened both eyes. That's when he saw another cloud form behind the first one, and then another, and another one after that. In all, there were nine clouds, one after another, in a straight line, starting at one end of the cavern and reaching to the other. To Brody, they looked like a row of big pillows, or giant cotton balls, or. . . .

"I got it," yelled Brody. "I know how we're going to get across the cavern."

Brody didn't explain his vision to the rest of SWEEPE. It might have seemed too dangerous, but to Brody, it made perfect sense. What represents the endless possibilities of your imagination more than clouds?

Brody slowly started backing away from the edge of the cliff until the distance felt right. He studied the clouds, just as he had so many times before on his many journeys with Grammy, and allowed his creativity to soar.

"He's not doing what I think he's doing?" Alec muttered. "Is he?"

"I think he might be," said Rosalina. She quickly turned to Jake. "You can't let him do this," but it was already too late.

All Jake and the rest of SWEEPE could do was watch as Brody Boondoggle ran with the speed of a cheetah and the courage of a lion straight for the edge of the cliff. At the perfect moment, Brody launched himself high in the air, right toward the middle of the very first cloud.

"Noooo," yelled Rosalina.

"Yes," answered Brody softly, because when his feet landed on the cloud, he didn't fall or drop or even tumble. Instead, he bounded high in the air, his arms swinging and his legs kicking as if he were on a soft, white trampoline with a just a hint of pink around the edges.

"Welcome to the Brodeo," Brody yelled with joy, twisting in midair so he could see the rest of SWEEPE. "Come on. Follow me."

"Can that be real?" asked Rosalina, watching Brody

laugh and bounce from cloud to cloud until he was literally on cloud nine (which some people call a place of perfect happiness).

"Only one way to find out," said Alec, who was the first to jump. He was followed closely by Rosalina, then Jake, and finally Punch. One by one, they each sprinted and launched and bounced and twisted and flipped and spun on cloud after cloud after cloud, traveling through the air in perfect happiness all the way to the other end of the cavern on trampolines made of clouds that no one could see.

Operation
Final Resort

Myles followed Felonious Fish like a great white shark follows an elephant seal, or an impatient Jake follows an instigating Brody, or a hungry osprey follows a sea trout right before the large bird with incredible eyesight and lightning speed swoops down and snags the unsuspecting fish right out of the water.

In this case, Myles wasn't looking to snag a fresh fish. He was going to steal Felonious' most prized possession.

Beep, beep, beep, beep.

Myles hated that noise just as much as Felonious Fish loved it. He couldn't stand the consistent, dull sound of the Rock Tracker that would continue to lead the

Scallywaggers from rock to rock until the Rock of Sarraka was finally back together.

They already had the first two pieces sealed and protected in a chamber that was impenetrable, meaning even if Myles wanted to steal the rocks or break them, he couldn't get to them. Not that he would want to break them, especially after being warned again and again by Felonious. "The rocks should be treated like eggs," Felonious kept saying, "because if they were chipped, even a little, the Pleasant Tree would wither away and so would Sarraka."

Okay, we get it. You've told us a million times, Myles wanted to say a million times.

And where was Brody Boondoggle? He had to be close, Myles figured, or at least he hoped. But even if Brody found his way to Sarraka, would he be any match for Rudy? Myles had overheard Felonious and Uncle Skeeta, so he knew Rudy already had two-thirds of Brody's powers, and Myles could see firsthand that Rudy knew how to use them, thanks to the elite spirit-animal skills he had learned from Felonious.

Rudy had mastered the art of belly breathing to

control his temperament and make his body powerful, calm, and centered. He could see with his third eye to truly connect with the auras and energy of Sarraka. And he used those connections, as well as his extraordinary new instincts, to communicate with the creatures of Sarraka, trying to convince them that Felonious was right and the Akaway was wrong—that the innocence and beauty and power of Sarraka needed to be protected, not shared with kids, who had proven time and time again that they didn't understand how to truly appreciate the power of their spirit animals.

Myles had done his best to delay the journey, but it wasn't good enough. So that evening, Myles didn't stay at the campsite with Rudy to shoot arrows or climb trees or tackle any of the obstacles naturally scattered throughout Sarraka. And he didn't hike the trails to brainstorm new ideas or look for inspiration with Uncle Skeeta. Instead, he came up with the plan for Operation Final Resort.

Step 1. Follow the fish.

When Felonious went for his nightly swim, Myles followed like a Canadian lynx follows a snowshoe hare, or a sleep-deprived Jake follows a particularly bothersome

Brody, or an Indian gray mongoose follows a king cobra, which only makes sense because the Indian gray mongoose is one of the few animals quick enough to catch the king cobra and also has a special ability to protect itself from the deadly snake's venom.

Felonious whistled the chorus of "Brownies for Breakfast," as he walked down the path to the pond. Myles waited from a safe distance while Felonious took the Rock Tracker from his finny pack, wrapped it in an oversized green leaf, and placed it next to a yellow lily with a single blue petal. A pretty good hiding place, thought Myles, and he noted the exact location.

While Myles waited, he wondered why he didn't think of this diversion sooner. It seemed so obvious now. You can't find rocks without a Rock Tracker.

Step 2. _Make your move._

Myles took a deep breath as Felonious slid into the water and started the same swimming routine that Myles had memorized—a brief warm-up near the surface to get used to the water, increase blood flow to the muscles and heart, and prepare his mind and spirit; an intense conditioning phase, consisting of powerful jumps in and out of the water, rapid sprints back and forth across the sea, and an extreme deep water dive to push his boundaries and test his limits; and finally, a calm and tranquil cooldown to lower his heart rate and reconnect with his surroundings.

Myles' heart beat faster when he saw Felonious start the deep water dive. He quickly scanned the area for witnesses, and when he saw none he darted down to the lily, grabbed the leaf, unwrapped the Rock Tracker, and placed it in the Hoodster.

Step 3. Cover your tracks.

Myles quickly snatched as many big, green leaves as he could find and wrapped each one around a pinecone. After pulling the lily from the ground, he placed the leaves randomly throughout the area.

Finally, he found a large branch that worked like a broom, and he brushed away his footprints as he left the scene of the crime like a golden jackal leaves a farm after it eats the sugarcane, or Jake sneaks out of Brody's room after a surprise attack, or a spider-eating assassin bug leaves a web after it has tricked the spider into thinking it was only a fly.

chapter
38

Nobody

Beep, beep, beep, beep.

It was a noise Myles hoped never to hear again. He checked the Rock Tracker that was now in his possession. It was still shut down, so the beeps had to be coming from somewhere else—from something else. By the time Myles realized that the dull, consistent beeping was actually coming from behind him, it was too late for Operation Run for Your Life, so Myles could only turn around and sigh when he saw Felonious holding a device that looked almost exactly like the one he had already stolen.

"The Rock-Tracker Tracker," Felonious announced with a shrug. "And if you managed to take this one, I would

have simply used the Rock-Tracker-Tracker Tracker."
Felonious changed to a more serious tone before adding,
"I don't know who you think you are, but nobody takes
my Rock Tracker."

For the first time in his life, Myles felt good as he
admitted, "Then I must be nobody." His mind raced,
searching for an escape, but the possibility faded when
Rudy appeared to his right, and Uncle Skeeta emerged
from the left.

"Listen, we don't want any trouble," said Rudy, as if he
were truly trying to help his new friend. "I'm sure there's
some logical explanation. Just give us back what is ours,
and nobody gets hurt."

Myles took a deep breath before reaching into his
Hoodster and slowly removing the Rock Tracker.

"Nice and easy," Felonious said calmly, and Myles
could hear the nervousness in his voice.

"Why should I give it to you?" blurted Myles. "So you
can destroy Sarraka?"

Felonious took one step closer to Myles, which caused
Myles to take two steps back.

"You haven't been paying close enough attention,"

said Felonious. "I'm not trying to destroy Sarraka. I'm trying to save it. I'm trying to protect it from all those kids who take, take, take, and never give back." He moved another step forward. "Don't you see? I love Sarraka. I might be the only one who loves it enough to do whatever it takes to save it."

"You'll do whatever it takes to get what you want," countered Myles. He flinched as Felonious took another step closer and motioned for Rudy and Uncle Skeeta to do the same.

"Stay where you are, or the Rock Tracker gets it," threatened Myles, holding the device high in the air. Felonious curled his fin in a ball to instruct Rudy and Uncle Skeeta to stay still.

"Listen, my friend," Felonious said calmly. "You can question our methods as much as you like, but you know I'm right. If we keep Sarraka open to the universe, all the resources will be gone before you can say Rock-Tracker Tracker. With my plan, the resources stay protected as they were meant to be." Felonious smiled like a salesfish. "There's enough power in Sarraka for all of us. And that means you, too."

"You're practically with us already," added Uncle Skeeta. "You came with us to find the first two pieces of the rock. Not many people get to see those rocks up close and personal. Can you imagine seeing all the rocks put back together again? The Rock of Sarraka in all its glory. You give us that Rock Tracker, and we'll make sure all your dreams come true."

"Come and join us," said Rudy, right on cue.

Myles didn't have to think for long. "I have an alternative suggestion," he said to Rudy. "Why don't you come with me?" He paused for a moment. "We'll go back and wait for Brody Boondoggle. We'll work with him to restore the Rock of Sarraka."

Rudy chuckled until he realized Myles wasn't joking. "Come on," suggested Myles. "They can't do this without you. And if you take over Sarraka by yourself, will it really be meaningful? Will it really be worth it if you're all by yourself?"

"Rudy won't be by himself—far from it," countered Felonious. "He will be the one everyone is talking about, the one with all the powers. If he listens to you, he'll continue to live in the shadow of that no-good, over-rated, two-faced, snot-nosed Brody Boondoggle." Felonious looked at Rudy. "Is that something you'd be interested in?"

We could say that Rudy's brain was spinning, that he was being pulled evenly in both directions, torn between continuing his mission with his team and doing the right thing with a new friend. We could say that, but we all know it wouldn't be true. The truth was Rudy didn't need to hear any speeches from Felonious. He wanted the power of Sarraka, and he knew in his heart that getting it was the only thing that mattered.

"Come on," Rudy repeated with a warm smile. He stuck out his hand, asking one more time for Myles to hand over the Rock Tracker before saying, "I thought we were friends."

If Rudy's spirit was starting to get just a little lighter through his journey in Sarraka, it reversed back toward the dark direction when Myles looked at Rudy and said, "You thought wrong."

Myles turned his head to Felonious and looked him right in the eye. Felonious didn't like the look of that stare. He knew what was going to happen next, and he was right. Myles flashed that devious grin that can only come from a spirit of a swift fox and hurled the Rock Tracker high in the air. Felonious jumped, but he was not a flying fish. The Rock Tracker soared over his head and smashed against the trunk of a giant sycamore tree, which made perfect sense because when Felonious saw the Rock Tracker shatter into a hundred pieces, he couldn't have been more sick.

Savage, Rudy whispered, as he watched Felonious and Uncle Skeeta rush to the aid of the shattered Rock Tracker. By the time they admitted that the Rock Tracker was unfixable, Myles had dashed away in the other direction. The Scallywaggers tried to follow his tracks, but they saw only the paw prints of a four-legged creature that could have been a deer or a wolf or just a swift fox.

"He's gone," said Rudy, plopping down on a rock.

"Don't worry about a thing. Here's what we're going to do," Felonious told Rudy, and Myles listened to the back-up plan from a hidden den in the ground. "It's like your Uncle Skeeta said: Find a way to win, no matter what," continued Felonious. "And this will be even better—because not only will we find the final piece of the rock, but we will also destroy Brody Boondoggle's spirit at the same time."

Not
the End of
the World

Now on the other side of the cavern, SWEEPE spent the greater part of the morning checking and searching and exploring their surroundings, looking for another bridge, a portal, or a waterslide—anything that could lead them to the magical world that seemed so close.

But nothing was there.

"We checked and double-checked this place from top to bottom," said Jake, pouring water on his bandana. "I hate to say it, but maybe this is where the adventure ends." If Jake hated to say it, Brody Boondoggle hated to hear it. He was exhausted, both mentally and physically, so he had little patience for a big brother who refused to see the magic.

"Thanks for that motivational speech," snapped Brody sarcastically. "Exactly what I would expect from someone who doesn't believe in anything." He dropped to one knee and took a deep breath. "This is where we're supposed to be," he said. "I can feel it."

"Feel what you want," said Jake, whipping the bandana at Brody. "I'm just saying, try using your brain instead of those fancy instincts sometimes. It was a good effort by everyone—even a little fun, if you don't take it too seriously. Maybe that's good enough. Maybe not finding a way into Sarraka right here, right now, isn't really the end of the world." He paused for a second so everyone could appreciate the "end of the world" joke. Rosalina and Punch offered token smiles, Alec rolled his eyes, and Brody groaned and mumbled that Jake was about as smart as a sponge.

And that's the way it went for a little while longer—a healthy mixture of disappointment and sorrow as, one by one, everyone realized that they had come as far as they could, and it still wasn't far enough. There was mostly silence, and every now and then someone tried to find the humor in the darkness, which doesn't always lead to magic, but usually leads to fun, especially for kids with strong connections to their spirit animals.

After all, it's not as if SWEEPE was stuck in school or even grounded for the weekend. They were outside, in an area that seemed as open and free as they imagined it would be in Sarraka. There was nothing they could do to stop the Scallywaggers, but there were still trees for climbing, water for swimming, and wide-open fields for running and playing or hanging out with your friends and sharing a moment of sadness.

It started when Jake and Alec noticed a bunch of random holes in the ground and couldn't resist inventing a game of gopher-hole billiards, which Alec won by rolling in three rocks in a row. Punching Crab joined in for a game of hide-and-seek, played completely in trees.

Brody and Rosalina were still devastated that the adventure seemed to be over or, at best, delayed, but they got up and agreed to search for another place nobody had ever seen before. They found a tranquil pond that was perfect for diving and splashing and cleansing their heartache away and invited the rest of SWEEPE to play games like ultimate water football, water balloon dodgeball, and "who can hold your breath the longest?" Brody focused on a sperm whale, which can stay underwater for ninety minutes, but since his powers were fading, he still only came in third.

The rest of the day was filled with the kind of love and laughter and lollygagging that can move the needle on a vitality meter in the perfect direction. They played hacky sack, horseshoes, and Capture the Flag. Jake even agreed to judge a sandcastle-building contest, which everybody won—except for Brody. That's the power of fun—sometimes it distracts you just enough to help you lighten up, get some perspective, and remember what's truly important.

By the time the sun went down, the five explorers were huddled in front of a roaring fire, eating s'mores, drinking root beer, and feeling good about their decision to spend one more night in nature before hiking back to Grammy's tomorrow.

"I wonder if Sarraka is really out there," whispered Rosalina after just the right amount of silence.

"I wonder how fast the fastest man would run on the moon," said Brody.

"I wonder how intelligent people can use *home* and *work* in the same sentence," said Alec.

"You know what I wonder?" said Jake, as he turned on his side to look at Punch. "How'd you get the name El Pantsing Crab?"

Punch shook his head, burned another marshmallow, and shoved it in his mouth. "No, no," he mumbled. "I'm feeling bad enough."

"Yes, yes," countered Brody. "No more delays." And since Jake and Brody were actually on the same side, Punching Crab acquiesced, which you may remember is a great word that means *agreed*.

Something Bigger

Punching Crab cleared his throat with a swig of root beer. He reached into his shell, pulled out the golden acorn, and held it up high for everyone to see. When he did, Brody could swear the fire roared just a little stronger, and the moon shined just a little brighter.

"Felonious gave me this golden acorn a long time ago," said Punching Crab. "It wasn't long after he and I met. I'll never forget it. He looked me in the eye and said, 'You are capable of great things, and so is this acorn.'"

"Wow, that doesn't sound like the Felonious I know," said Alec.

"Well, people change," said Punching Crab.

"It would be nice if they could change back," said Brody.

"Do you think it's possible?" asked Rosalina.

Brody thought for just long enough to give Jake a chance to notice the anticipation in Rosalina's eyes, meaning Jake knew she needed to believe, even if he didn't. "Anything is possible," Jake shrugged. Rosalina nodded and smiled.

Punching Crab passed the acorn around for everyone to hold, see, and touch. When it got to Brody, his hand burned, and he could feel his right eye start to tingle as if the last of the remaining pink was trying to make one last fight for control.

"So what does that have to do with El Pantsing Crab?" asked Rosalina.

"Everything," said Punch. He snatched the acorn back from Brody and explained that when he learned that Felonious had teamed up with Uncle Skeeta and Rudy and betrayed the Akaway, he felt lost and alone. So he clung to the first thing that always gave him hope—the golden acorn.

"If it's so important, how come you never mentioned this golden acorn before?" asked Jake.

"I guess I didn't think that far ahead," responded Punch. "But trust me, I carried it around with me all the time, and when I was at my lowest, I squeezed the acorn tight, looking for hope. Next thing I knew, I saw a golden toad hop on a bus, and I knew I had to follow it."

Punch explained that he had traveled for nine days, covering more than three thousand miles. For most of his journey, he was curled up in a ball, as if his heart was trying to convince his brain that what he had witnessed at the Sequestered Spring never happened. The problem was that the only thing Punching Crab had was the golden acorn and the hope it represented. And hope can't buy you food, shelter, or sunglasses. He was hungry and tired. A young boy offered to share his peanut butter and banana sandwich. "But you have to give me that golden acorn," the little boy said.

Punch refused, and, for the next week, he ate only the pickles he picked from the garbage on the bus.

When he was looking for a place to stay in Mexico, a local motel offered a free room in exchange for the golden acorn. Punch refused, and he was forced to sleep on the sandy shores of Siesta Beach.

Punching Crab was desperate. He would do anything for sleep, shelter, and more pickles. Then one day when Punch was on the beach, a teenage boy misread the sign Punching Crab was holding.

"You'll pants for pickles?" the boy said.

The sign actually read, *I'll dance for pickles*, but it was close enough for Punch.

The boy pointed to a large, hairy man. "That's my brother-in-law," he said. "Get him."

With only pickles on his mind, Punch snuck up to his target, looked both ways, grabbed the man's pants with both claws, and pulled them down. His customer loved it. Word spread, and, pretty soon, everyone wanted to hire the new crab in town.

"That's when I turned into the notorious El Pantsing Crab," he admitted.

Things were going well for a while, but then Punch got sloppy and pantsed an undercover police officer. When he got caught, the policeman offered to let him off with a warning in exchange for the golden acorn, but Punch refused and was sent to jail.

"I always thought this acorn was going to be the key

to something bigger," Punch said. He stood up and walked closer to the fire. "Now I see that it's really been the cause of all my problems." He squeezed it tight one more time. "You know something?" he said. "I'm done with this acorn. I've been waiting and waiting for something extraordinary to happen, and look where it's gotten me." Then he threw the golden acorn into the fire.

A split second later, something extraordinary did happen. A sharp burst of light shot up into the sky as if it were connecting with the moon. Beams of light shot back down from all the stars, the fire roared into the heavens, and smoke circled from the fire like a tornado.

Brody looked at Punch. "It was the acorn," he said. "You had the magic all the time." Brody's eye got bright, and his path was clearer now than ever before.

"Everyone follow me," he said. And that's what they did, diving right through the portal of smoke, out of the Grappling Mountains, and into the world of Sarraka.

Part III
The Escape Out

Short and Secretive

Brody Boondoggle rested his hand on the rich Sarraka soil and listened to the rhythms of the land flowing through the ground.

THUMP, thump, thump, thump.

That's when he heard a familiar voice deep inside. It was the Akaway saying hello and welcome and providing the exact location for the final piece of the rock. Punching Crab and Alec and even Jake were ready to roll, but there was something different about Rosalina, who was still like a statue, simply staring into the distance.

"What's going on?" asked Brody, placing his hand on Rosalina's shoulder. "We need to move."

Rosalina nodded, but she didn't move. Instead, she transferred her gaze to Brody and the rest of SWEEPE before calmly explaining exactly what she saw. A short and secretive conversation followed, and when it was done, they all agreed that Rosalina's instincts just might be right. To truly succeed, Brody's next journey would be one that he needed to take on his own.

chapter 42

A Blobfish Out of Water

"You look worse than a blobfish out of water."

They were the first words Brody had heard in the several hours he walked alone through the hills and valleys of Sarraka. And he wasn't the least bit surprised when he turned and learned that those words were coming from his ex-best friend Rudy, who actually looked just the opposite. Rudy seemed strong and confident, and Brody could tell he was ready for a fight—mostly because Rudy was wearing a black baseball hat that read, "Ready for a fight."

"I see you finally made it. Took you long enough," said Rudy, with a cocky grin. "Where's your lame big brother and the rest of your so-called friends? Too afraid to come with you?"

"Not afraid," said Brody. "Just smart. This was supposed to be a secret mission, and it's harder to track someone who's traveling alone."

"Well, you're not as smart as you think," Rudy continued, circling Brody like a shark. "I've been tracking you for miles, and you didn't even realize it." Rudy paused for a moment to let his power sink in. He wanted Brody to know that he was stronger, faster, and smarter. "I know the Akaway told you the location of the final piece of the rock. I know that's where you're headed now. And now you're all alone. Great job on the secret mission," Rudy added sarcastically.

"It seemed like a good idea at the time," admitted Brody with a shrug. He scanned the area. "What about you? Where's Uncle Skeeta and Felonious?"

"As soon as they saw that you were alone, I convinced them to wait at the Pleasant Tree," said Rudy. "Don't worry, you'll see them soon enough." Rudy took a step closer to Brody. "After all," he added, "This is between you and me."

Brody took a deep breath. He actually *felt* like a

blobfish out of water—weak and tired and a little concerned that Rudy now possessed two-thirds of his powers. But the blobfish looks like it does for a reason. It might not be what many consider pretty, but its appearance helps it explore deep parts of the water and go places other creatures can't. In that same way, Brody was ready to go and do whatever it took to save a world that desperately needed him.

"I guess we have nothing else to talk about," shrugged Brody. He waved his arms as he started to walk further along the gravel path. "Follow me. This is going to be fun."

Together Brody and Rudy walked for just a short distance. They talked very little except to say things like, "It doesn't have to be like this," or "I think I'll stay in Sarraka awhile once I take over," or "Did you know that an apple, potato, and onion all taste the same if you eat them with your eyes closed and nose plugged?"

When they turned around a bend and saw an open field, Brody pointed to the tall, narrow structure way off in the distance. On top of the structure balanced a wide, flat platform. From afar, it seemed like a giant chessboard balancing on an enormous pencil.

"It's called the Teeter Attack, because the platform is teetering back and forth in the wind," Brody explained. "You see that?"

"If you can see it, I can see it twice as well," said Rudy, who was familiar with these types of adventure challenges that were scattered throughout Sarraka. "And I would call it the X-treme Teeter Attack."

Boy, I guess he has twice my ego, too, Brody thought, and he secretly wondered if this was the kind of thing that bothered Jake so much. Could he be that annoying? It was even more irritating that Rudy was right—using an *X* did make the challenge seem cooler.

"There's a wooden box in the middle of that platform, and in the box is a very special rock," continued Brody, calmly. "Whoever gets it first . . . ," Brody paused and shrugged. "Well, you know what's at stake."

The X-treme Teeter Attack

The dash to the X-treme Teeter Attack was not easy—nothing that important ever was. Rudy concentrated on a brown hare, which might be small but is just as fast as a cheetah, and bolted into the grassy field. Brody stayed close behind by combining the spirit of a wildebeest with a competitive spirit that comes naturally to almost anyone with an older brother.

Toughen up.

By the time Rudy and Brody arrived at the base of the tower, they had been pricked by the spiky needles of blue spruce trees and stung by the burrs of a cocklebur plant (its real name is Xanthium Strumarium, but why would you ever use that name when you can say *cocklebur?*), and they were now covered from head to toe in rich, dark Sarraka-style mud, which they purposefully rolled in to soothe the pain from the prickles and the burrs, and also to get muddy.

Brody was breathing a little heavier than he wanted to admit, especially compared with Rudy, who had already started climbing the hundred-foot rock tower by just thinking of a gecko and the superfine hairs on its feet.

Brody concentrated on a tree frog and the sticky mucus it produces while he tried to follow Rudy up the rock. The problem was that tree frogs struggle on dry, rough surfaces, a fact Brody would have known had he been at full strength, so by the time he finally reached the top, Rudy had already spotted the wooden box in the middle of the flat square and made his first move to capture it.

But when he sprang for the box, Rudy's weight caused the platform to teeter so severely that he fell on his belly and started sliding off the surface, which was as slick as coconut oil. Just as he was about to slide off the side, Rudy caught the end of the safety ledge with his left hand and hung in the air.

"That doesn't look so good," Brody said from the ledge on the other side of the platform.

"You think you could do better?" Rudy replied, as he regained his grip with his right hand and pulled himself to safety.

Before Brody could answer, he was distracted by a loud, rolling sound. It was a boulder about the size of a baby elephant, rolling around on the platform, in and out, back and forth, in no particular pattern.

Brody could see Rudy's mind churning, thinking of all the possibilities. Brody tried to do the same. How do you overcome a platform that teeters with any movement, a floor so slippery any mistake could lead to a hundred-foot fall, and, finally, a boulder created to protect the exact box you are trying to snatch?

There was only one way, and Brody and Rudy both knew it. They glared at each other, nodded, and, at the same time, sprang onto the platform. It was more relief than happiness when they realized their plan was actually working. They were acting as a counterbalance, working as equal weights on opposite sides of the platform. If someone moved right, the other person would move left to keep the platform perfectly balanced.

In a strange way, they were actually forced to work together, the way they used to when they were the best kind of best friends—the kind that stuck up for each other, looked out for each other, and were always in it together.

Now, with their arms out as if they were surfing, Brody and Rudy seemed to be connected in that same way. Together, they watched the boulder circle around the platform once, then again. Together, they could tell it had a pattern, a rhythm. When it rolled a few feet toward Brody, Rudy knew immediately to back away. When the boulder slid across to the other side, Brody took two quick steps toward the center to keep the platform in perfect balance. Together, they waited the exact amount of time before taking another step toward the center of the square.

And that's the way it was, like a beautiful dance between two X-best friends who, for a few moments, understood maybe an *X* in front doesn't always make everything cooler. Two steps up, one step back, slide, slide, slide. One step over, two steps back, slide, slide, slide.

Maybe they didn't even realize they were working

together, or maybe they just didn't want to admit it, but soon it was obvious they had mastered the rhythms of the board, the boulder, and each other.

There was no rush, and there were no excuses. They took no chances, because they couldn't afford to. They were in too deep, up too high, and they had to trust each other now more than ever. One sudden movement, and the boulder would slide the wrong way or the board would teeter, and they could easily slide off the edge.

Then, just as Brody and Rudy moved the exact right amount to almost make it to the box that contained the rock that they wanted so desperately, Rudy paused, and a cocky smile appeared on his face. Brody cringed.

"What's going on inside that head of yours?" asked Brody suspiciously.

"Exactly what you think," answered Rudy. "This is called the Teetering Attack, not the Teetering Teammates. I'm grabbing the final piece of the rock. I'm winning this race. I'm capturing my destiny."

"If you go for the rock now, the boulder will crush you," said Brody. "Do you want that to be your destiny? The boy who got crushed like a bug?"

It wasn't a bug Rudy was thinking of. It was a mantis shrimp, which uses a compressed body to take off as fast as a speeding bullet. And so that's exactly what Rudy did.

chapter 44

Predictable

Rudy's eyes grew wide, and his face turned white, which is a common reaction when there's a boulder the size of a baby elephant steamrolling in your direction. Brody had two choices: He could either watch Rudy get rolled or do what he did—dash back exactly three-and-a-half steps and stomp down with the weight of a water buffalo, which, in Brody's current condition, only had the effect of stomping down with the weight of a warthog. But that was enough to cause the platform to shift just enough to make the boulder roll off course and miss Rudy by a brown hare.

Rudy opened his eyes and let out a deep sigh.

"You're so predictable, I almost feel bad," said Rudy, meaning he knew exactly what Brody was going to do. In fact, he had counted on it. Then Rudy smirked a little wider when he saw the same boulder that barely missed him rolling straight for Brody.

"Just take a step back," Brody instructed, but Rudy was predictable, too.

"Man, if I were rooting for you, I'd be really mad right now," taunted Rudy, "because I'm not going to help you. And you should have known that."

That left Brody to dive out of the way of the boulder, causing the platform to teeter so much that Brody fell on his belly and slid down with the boulder following close behind.

As he approached the edge of the platform, Brody lunged to hold on with one hand in the same way Rudy had done. That move was harder than it looked, and Brody's strength betrayed him. Luckily, the spirit animals didn't, or at least not the extinct ones.

Just a second into Brody's free fall, he felt the sharp talons of a winged lizard from 145 million years ago grab his shirt and bring him safely to the ground.

"Thank you," he whispered to the pterodactyl, who crowed back as if to say, "Sorry I couldn't get there sooner. I came from very far away."

With the box sealed securely in his arm, Rudy took one more step to the center of the square, the only place that was safe at all times, and waited for the platform to correct itself. He took three quick breaths to properly unite his courage and his strength, and then he started running at full speed.

When the platform started to tilt, Rudy lunged forward, gaining more and more momentum, until he shot off the side of the tower. At the same time, he opened his arms like a flying squirrel and rode the wind safely to the ground.

Savage.

"You were right. That was fun," said Rudy with a satisfying grin as he stood over Brody like a vulture. He might have wondered if the "fun" gave Sarraka a little more time and energy, but that didn't matter anymore. He had what he came for. He had outsmarted Brody, and all that was left was to return to the Pleasant Tree, reconnect the pieces of the Rock of Sarraka, and capture its powers.

"You want to come, don't you?" predicted Rudy, who understood that the only thing better than defeating Brody was having Brody there to see it happen. "You never know, you might enjoy it."

Perfect Click

The Pleasant Tree was everything Brody Boondoggle had ever imagined, even if Uncle Skeeta and Felonious Fish were waiting just a few feet away when he and Rudy arrived. Brody actually seemed calm and relaxed as Rudy placed the special wooden box in the soft grass next to Felonious, who was double-checking *The Secrets of Sarraka* to make sure he knew the exact way to reconnect the three pieces of the rock.

Felonious returned the notebook to his finny pack, but as he turned to pick up the final piece of the rock from Rudy, another cold chill came over his body. In that moment, Felonious didn't *think* he was being watched anymore. He *knew* it. The feeling was getting stronger, closer, and more real than ever. Felonious took a few deep breaths to try to contain his emotions, but it only made him see things more clearly.

The nothingness was coming. This was his last chance to stop whatever it was, and time was running out. Felonious possessed the final piece of the rock and was under the shade of the Pleasant Tree. All he had to do was connect the pieces, and he would control Sarraka. He would close the portal to the outside world once and for all. Kids would no longer be connected to their spirit animals, and the nothingness that haunted his vision would be shut out of Sarraka before it was too late.

Felonious refocused his attention as he removed the first two pieces of the rock from their protective containers. He immediately felt greatness in these rocks, and beads of sweat started to form on his gills as he slowly turned the rocks slightly this way and that way until there was a perfect connection.

CLICK.

Felonious exhaled. He was halfway there.

"Hand me the final rock," he said, his voice quivering.

Rudy slid open the top of the wooden box and reached inside. Like a doctor holding a new baby, he gently passed Felonious the last rock. Felonious studied it from every angle—twisting, probing, examining, and reexamining.

"Is there a problem?" asked Uncle Skeeta.

Felonious didn't answer. He was too focused on the rock. He didn't sense the greatness. He flipped it over and slowly moved the final piece closer and closer until it touched the other two rocks softly and perfectly. But there was no perfect click—or even an imperfect one. Panicked and confused, Felonious started jamming the rock furiously into the first two pieces. Still no click.

"Welcome to the Brodeo," Brody said, and he couldn't resist flashing that cocky grin, even though he promised himself he wouldn't. He beamed, but he was met with only blank stares because the Scallywaggers had no idea what he meant. Brody shook his head and rolled his eyes. "Did you ever consider that *that* rock might not be *the* rock you're looking for?"

chapter
46

Worth
the Risk

When Brody Boondoggle and the rest of SWEEPE first
arrived in Sarraka, the plan was simple: find the final
piece of the rock, restore the balance of power, and defeat
the Scallywaggers once and for all. But then Rosalina saw
something in the distance, and everything changed.

That something was a note from Myles welcoming his
"little sister" to Sarraka and providing all the important
information that he had gathered about the Scallywaggers.
He told her about *The Secrets of Sarraka*, described Rudy's
new powers, and warned her about their strategy to follow
Brody Boondoggle to the final piece of the rock.

SWEEPE had a short and secretive conversation, which
led to a new plan that was not so simple.

First, they quickly gathered enough wood to build a small, sturdy box, which was just the right size to hold a very special rock. Second, they teamed up with a flock of Carolina parakeets, which were hunted for their colorful feathers and had been extinct for more than a hundred years. The small but pesky birds gladly agreed to carry the box to the top of the Teetering Attack.

Brody would head off in one direction, making just enough noise and leaving just the right amount of clues to be easily followed. The rest of SWEEPE would sneak off in the other direction, trusting their instincts and their spirit animals, until they reached a secret location that was almost impossible to find without a Rock Tracker or an Akaway.

"They'll never suspect a thing," said Brody, and he was right. After all, it takes a rare and special power to retrieve or even touch the Rock of Sarraka. Only a few people had that power, and if anyone else tried, they could lose their spirit animals or worse.

"That's why you have to do it," said Brody, pointing to the one person who made perfect sense. And all eyes turned to the girl with long dark hair and glasses.

"Me?" answered Rosalina softly, and Brody nodded, because it seemed so clear. There was something about Rosalina that made her different, different but good. She dreamed of places nobody had ever seen before. She could see animals that didn't exist. When the world was particularly crazy, she was curiously calm. She was even born on the right day for magic.

"Are you sure?" asked Rosalina.

"The question is, are you?" replied Brody, and then he simply shrugged, smiled, and walked away.

Rosalina barely had time to consider the question. It hadn't been long since she was at an all-time low, sitting at her desk in a Mexican prison, but that seemed like a lifetime ago. She had come so far, and yet she was never more scared. What if she wasn't the right person? What if she failed? What if she lost her new spirit animal? What if? What if? What if?

Still, after a treacherous hike filled with danger, surprises, and more danger, Rosalina stood on the edge of the Hidden Pond at the exact location that the Akaway had described. She was still nervous and still scared, but she was never more excited. "I'm sure," she whispered to the sky, because she knew deep down inside that Brody would hear her.

Rosalina spread her arms and fell back into the warm and mysterious water. She was gone for ten seconds, twenty seconds, one minute, two minutes. It seemed much longer to Jake, who was about to dive in when Rosalina appeared on a sandbar on the other side of the pond with a huge smile on her face and a clear rock so pure that it seemed it was nothing more than a jagged ball full of air.

Now, to the absolute shock of Felonious, Uncle Skeeta, and Rudy, Rosalina and the rest of SWEEPE emerged from around the bend like a pack of African wild dogs, which as a group are some of the most efficient hunters in the world. Rosalina removed the final rock from a specially made protective bag and proudly handed it to Brody.

Maybe it was the rock, maybe it was seeing Rosalina and the rest of his friends once again, or maybe it was some combination of both, but regardless, almost immediately the pink in Brody's right eye returned, and his focus was perfectly clear. He felt stronger—as if the basketball could now bounce or the tires on the three-wheeled bike were now filled with air or the spirit of the Akaway was being restored.

"You're no ordinary girl, are you?" asked Felonious. Brody answered for her, "There's no such thing."

With that, Brody focused all his energy on the powers of the Akaway, and when he did, the first two pieces of the rock started to roll in Felonious' fins. Like a magnet, they were being drawn to the final, and most powerful, piece of the rock. Felonious tried to hold on tight, but he was no match for the powers of Sarraka.

Unfortunately, Rudy was.

As the rocks floated through the air on a direct course to Brody, Rudy dashed to intersect the path and snatch the rocks in midair. He held the rocks like hostages, daring anyone to make a move. Then Rudy placed the rocks in his pockets, smiled, and nodded, and started doing the one thing that made everyone realize that defeating the bad guys is never as easy as you think.

chapter
47

Backup Plan

It was the sarcastic clap, and Rudy was executing the movement perfectly, just as his Uncle Skeeta had done at the Sequestered Spring. He started with just one clap. There was a long pause, and then there was another clap and another long pause.

"Very nice job, everyone," began Rudy, because everyone knows that sarcastic claps aren't nearly as effective if they're not followed by an annoying speech. "I hope you're happy. You did what you had to do. You found your way back to Sarraka. And that was a pretty tricky plan leading us away from the real rock." He looked at Rosalina. "We would have never believed there was someone else out there capable of handling such power, but I guess we were wrong."

Rosalina shrugged. "I guess so."

"No worries," continued Rudy. "You did what you had to do, and now so will I."

Rudy removed the two rocks from his pockets, held them in his hands like cymbals, and flashed the cocky smile that he now seemed to share with Brody. He thought of a martial eagle, which is the largest and most powerful eagle in Africa, and, in a single motion, started moving his wings together, an action that would certainly crack the rocks and set off a chain reaction that would destroy Sarraka forever.

"Stop."

The word could have easily come from Brody, Punch, or any member of SWEEPE, because it was exactly what they were all thinking. But that's not who made the desperate plea. It was coming from the one person who had always been on Rudy's side. That is, until he spent enough time in a magical world to maybe see things just a little bit differently.

"If you break those rocks, Sarraka will be no more,"

Uncle Skeeta said in a calm and soothing voice. "Why would you want to do something like that?"

Rudy just stared him in the eye and said, "Because that's what you taught me to do."

Uncle Skeeta's bushy eyebrows rose in surprise. "I never taught you to *destroy* Sarraka," he said.

"Maybe not exactly," clarified Rudy. "But you taught me to make sure there's always a way to win. You taught me to always have a backup plan. If we could have controlled the power of Sarraka, we would have won. But it's clearly not going to be that easy. But we can still win. You can still control the kids. Felonious can still make sure kids are never again connected to their spirit animals. I can still defeat Brody Boondoggle. We can still make sure our dreams come true."

"That's not a dream," said Punching Crab. "It's a nightmare." He turned to Felonious. "I know you," said Punch. "You could never destroy Sarraka. You love it too much."

Felonious nodded. He seemed scared and worn out. "You're right, my friend," he said, which provided about one second of relief that quickly vanished when Felonious pointed to Rudy and added, "I do love Sarraka. And that's why it must be destroyed."

Destroying Sarraka

Felonious didn't perform a sarcastic clap, but he did tell a story. It was a story about the feeling he had had since the Rock of Sarraka split into three pieces. The eerie, cold feeling that Felonious hoped wasn't real. It wasn't until he finally held the first two rocks that he knew for sure that it was very real indeed. He could see that something, or more accurately, *nothing* was coming.

This nothingness was not coming to share Sarraka, like Brody and the Akaway wanted to do, and it wasn't coming to protect Sarraka from kids and outsiders like Felonious envisioned. It wasn't even coming to destroy Sarraka, the way Felonious and Rudy planned to do now.

No, holding the rocks allowed Felonious to see that this nothingness wanted to capture Sarraka alive, so it could absorb its power—pollute the water, destroy the forests, and hunt the animals until there was nothing left to take. It would be worse than anything Punching Crab could imagine.

"And I cannot bear to see that happen to a place I love," said Felonious.

"So you'd rather destroy it yourself?" yelled Rosalina. "That doesn't make any sense."

"It makes all the sense in the world," said Felonious. "If we destroy Sarraka now, it will be clean, natural, organic, on its own terms. But if we allow this nothingness to take over, Sarraka will turn into something it was never meant to be. There will be long, drawn-out suffering like you've never imagined."

Felonious understood that he was a fish who would never be trusted again, especially not by Punch and the rest of SWEEPE, who looked at him with outrage and anger. So before he said another word, he simply turned to Brody Boondoggle, pointed to his right eye, and told him to look for the truth.

"Do you see it?" Felonious finally asked after just a few minutes. "I know you do, because there is no one more connected than you."

Punch, Jake, Alec, Rosalina, and even Uncle Skeeta stared at Brody, hoping he would say that Felonious was desperate and devious and not telling the truth. "Go ahead," Felonious repeated. "Tell me I'm wrong."

But Brody couldn't lie. Because when he looked with his pink eye and truly connected with the world he loved, he saw the same nothingness coming their way. Even Rosalina could sense the truth. "Your dream," she said to Brody. "Turns out it was a bad dream after all."

Brody stared at Felonious. "Tell me how to stop it," he demanded.

The confirmation of his fears hit Felonious like a punch in the gills. Even he had wished he was wrong.

"You don't get it," warned Felonious. "There is no stopping it. If this nothingness arrives, it will take over Sarraka as easily as a lion overtakes a zebra, or a bear catches a fish, or a swift fox snatches a rabbit."

"We stopped you," growled Alec, the badger in him ready to attack. "Is this nothingness stronger than you?"

Felonious just shook his head as if there were no comparison. "Much stronger," he admitted. "And it's stronger than the Akaway, too." Felonious dipped his head. For the first time in a long time, he felt almost bad for the kids. He had not only stolen their hopes, but he had also taken their purpose as well. What was the point of saving Sarraka if it was only going to be tortured and destroyed?

"Whatever I have done, it was in the name of love," said Felonious softly. "And I'm telling you, if you truly love Sarraka, then the only way to protect it is to destroy it now, once and for all. And that's what we're going to do."

Felonious nodded to Rudy, who once again raised his arms, lifting the rocks back above his head. Without wasting another second, Rudy crashed the rocks together with force and fury, creating a deafening sound that echoed throughout the land, as if to alert every living animal, vegetable, and mineral that Sarraka would soon be no more.

The Sarraka Blues

The ground started to vibrate, the sky got dark, and the winds started whipping around like a miniature tornado. And then it stopped. A few moments later, it happened again, only this time it was a little bit stronger.

"Duck," pointed Punching Crab, and everyone looked as a kamikaze duck came flying by.

"These are preliminary shock waves," explained Felonious, advising everyone to remain on the ground and cover their heads until the second tremor ended. While they did, he added that shock waves are very common when there's an underground explosion, and that they would keep getting a little worse each time.

"Until when?" asked Rosalina.

Felonious paused and took a deep breath. "Until the end."

Felonious removed the vitality meter from his pocket and observed the needle moving quickly to the left, completely out of the green section and into the red. "Trust me," he added, throwing the device to Brody to prove his point. "You couldn't save Sarraka if you wanted to. There's no time."

Felonious sprang to his tail and pulled two small branches from the Pleasant Tree, which was clearly starting to weaken. Its leaves fell to the ground, fungus appeared on the branches, and a long crack started to form on the trunk.

Felonious rubbed the branches together so quickly that a small fire started. He grabbed the golden acorn from his finny pack and dropped it into the fire, producing a perfect wall of smoke.

"We're leaving," said Felonious. "And if you were smart, you would come with us."

Brody looked at Rosalina, who looked at Alec, who looked at Jake, who looked at Punch, and with each look, their decision to stay grew stronger and more obvious. Felonious just shook his head. "Suit yourselves," he said. "I'm sorry it had to be this way."

A few moments later, the wall of smoke grew taller, and Rudy and Uncle Skeeta stepped next to Felonious, ready to return to the safety of their own world.

"You just won't give up," Rudy said to Brody.

"I guess not," shrugged Brody.

"You still don't know what you believe in, do you?" Uncle Skeeta said to Jake.

"If you say so," Jake replied.

"I'm sorry you'll never be a spirit animal," Felonious said to Punching Crab.

Punching Crab sighed deeply and rubbed his eyes with his claws. There was still a little acorn of hope inside him that wanted to believe in Felonious, to thank him for introducing a small crab to such a magnificent world. Anything was possible. Punch was sure of it, and that was partially because of the Felonious he used to know.

Punch shook his head, thought for a moment, and knew what he had to do next. He walked over to his old friend and mentor and gave him a big, fat hug. It was something Felonious never expected and never forgot. Then Felonious, Uncle Skeeta, and Rudy disappeared into the wall of smoke.

chapter 50

He's Both

As Brody sat on the ground with chaos and craziness going on all around him, he actually smiled, because at that point he remembered the one spirit who would know exactly what to do when the Rock of Sarraka was broken and the magical world was crumbling around you.

"Follow me," Brody yelled, as a third tremor erupted. He scooped up all the pieces of the rocks and carefully placed them in their protective bags. Then he followed his instincts, sprinting through the valleys and trails of Sarraka on his way back to the safety of the Aka Lair.

But this tremor was worse than the other two. The sky

became darker, and the winds blew harder, causing trees to tip over, water levels to rise and wash onto shore, and twigs, branches, and everything else that wasn't secured to fly uncontrollably through the air.

The last hundred yards felt like a giant game of dodgeball, and SWEEPE was losing. A large rock hammered Jake in the leg. He had to crawl on his belly to finally reach the cave. A garden snake flew through the air like a ninja whip and tied itself around Alec's legs. He had to hop the final stretch to meet Jake. Punch was zigging and zagging as if he were being chased by a bear, but he looked more like a pinball, bouncing off rocks and trees until he finally reached the cave. A branch twisted off a nearby tree and was about to smash Rosalina, but Brody quickly dove and knocked her out of the way. Rosalina was safe, but the branch struck Brody in the ribs.

"Crack."

Brody fell to the ground in agony. Alec, Punch, and Jake watched from the safety of the cave as Rosalina tried to help Brody. "I can barely breathe," he wheezed.

The conditions continued to get worse as Rosalina tried harder to lift Brody to his feet, pulling with all her might, until finally Jake limped out of the cave and slung Brody's right arm over his shoulder while Rosalina did the same with the left.

"Man, you need to toughen up," Jake said, as he dropped Brody at the entrance of the cave. He nodded to Rosalina, "Awesome job by you."

Brody took just a second to catch his breath. While the rest of SWEEPE pushed rocks and boulders in front of the opening of the cave for extra protection, Brody crawled to the back of the cave where the Akaway was struggling to keep Sarraka alive. Brody looked at the Akaway with intense appreciation, meaning he knew she had given so much of herself so others could grow and thrive and imagine. In a way, she was like the sun, the source of energy for kids, for animals, for Sarraka.

Brody took a deep breath because he knew the Akaway was listening. He knew Rosalina was listening, too. She was hiding around the corner, but Brody sensed that she was there, and something about it felt right. If this was the end of this adventure, Rosalina should be part of it. After all, she had been there when it started.

Brody thought about his next words carefully.

"I don't know what to do," Brody whispered to the Akaway. "Does it make sense to risk everything to save a magical world just so something darker can destroy it?"

Rosalina listened anxiously. Part of her wanted to jump out and stand with Brody, and the other part realized it was not her place—at least not yet. So she stood silently while Brody waited for an answer, a voice deep inside his soul that would give him direction, an insight into what to do next.

But this time, the voice never came. Instead, a warm glow swept over Brody's body. He looked over his shoulder and smiled.

"What is it?" blurted out Rosalina, who couldn't stand the suspense.

"Come see for yourself," said Brody.

Rosalina's eyes filled with tears when she peeked her head around the corner and saw all the friends that had helped them along the way. Not the members of SWEEPE, but their other friends—the passenger pigeon, the Falkland Island wolf, the laughing owl, the pterodactyl, the Carolina parakeets. And then, one more very important friend emerged.

"Myles," Rosalina said softly as if this were just a dream.

"Myles is a swift fox?" asked Brody. "I thought he was your brother."

Rosalina gave Myles a big hug. "He's both," said Rosalina, and suddenly everything made sense—why Myles was drawn to Sarraka, how he saw the Grappling Mountains in his dreams, why he fled the prison at that exact time he was needed most, why La Tarántula never went after him, and how he had entered Sarraka, communicated with the Akaway, and escaped the Scallywaggers on four legs instead of two.

It was because Myles was not a kid at all. He was a rare and beautiful animal, caught between worlds and battling extinction by hiding out with a caring and loving person, who had the gift to see animals only few people could.

Of course, Rosalina saw Myles as a smart and curious spirit, and there was an instant connection—as close as any brother and sister could ever have. Myles gave Rosalina inspiration and the vision to see a world beyond the prison walls. And Rosalina gave Myles protection and family so he would never truly feel extinct.

Then one day, Myles couldn't ignore his calling

anymore. A voice told him he was needed elsewhere, and that voice triggered a vision of a bigger purpose. So Myles left La Casa Sin Salida the same way he came, quietly, without anybody but Rosalina knowing or caring.

But before he did, he made sure Rosalina wouldn't be alone. He told her about the Grappling Mountains and watched her paint them on the wall as an inspiration to keep dreaming. He made sure his fellow extinct animals would bring a unique young man into her life. And he inspired her so that when the time was right, she would believe anything was possible.

And then he went to fulfill his destiny. Myles was the one creature that was clever enough to get into Sarraka, cunning enough to take the form of a 12-year-old boy, convincing enough to combat the Scallywaggers just enough to give Brody a chance, and courageous enough to risk the one relationship that meant the most to him, because he knew, if everything went right, they would be together again.

And now, here they were, just as Myles had hoped.

"It was you the whole time," said Rosalina, staring at Myles. "You made this happen."

"Not really," said Myles. "It was all of us." He motioned to his fellow animals, his new family. "This is our home. This was our one chance to do whatever we could to save it."

Rosalina thought for a moment. "One chance?" she repeated, and a chill came across her body when she finally understood what that meant. "You're not coming back with me," she said, as a tear streamed down her cheek. Myles shifted his gaze back to Brody Boondoggle.

"There is good on your side," he said, as Jake, Alec, and Punching Crab entered the chamber. And just like that, Brody knew what to do next. It was too late to help these animals save their species, but he could still help them save their home, and that's what everyone agreed to do.

That was until a loud, deep ringing echoed through the cave. At first, Brody thought it was another tremor, but it was worse. It was the vitality meter that Felonious had tossed to Brody, the one that could determine exactly how much life was left in Sarraka.

Brody reached into his pocket, and when he flipped open the device, the needle had moved almost all the way to the left into an area called "the wasteland."

"How much time do we have?" asked Rosalina, cautiously.

The expression on his face said it all. But the word still stung like a bullet ant, which is considered to have the most painful sting in the insect world, when Brody just looked up and answered, "None."

Butterfly

La Tarántula slumped next to Grammy on the big red couch. She stared blankly at the wall, trying to think of an answer to Grammy's latest question: "What makes you happy?" It was Grammy's way of cheering her up. After all, if you think of things that make you happy, you just might start to feel a little happier.

"I used to love to dance," La Tarántula conceded with a deep surrendering sigh. Grammy glanced at her oddly, trying to figure out why anyone would bring a glove to France, but before she could ask, La Tarántula spoke again, this time in a louder voice so that even Grammy could hear. "We used to play music as loud as we could and just

let our bodies go loco." She smiled. "Fue muy divertido."
And Grammy smiled back, because she understood that
it meant, "It was so much fun."

Then La Tarántula's smile melted away. "I can't
remember the last time I had that kind of fun."

Grammy stood up, grabbed La Tarántula's hand, and
dragged her down the stairs into the front yard.

"You shouldn't have to," Grammy said with a wink.
"Espera aquí."

La Tarántula "waited here," as Grammy had asked, and
a few moments later, Grammy emerged from the garage
with two large speakers and a pair of tall wooden boxes.
Tackle, who had spent the afternoon playing with a few of
the feral cats who lived under the house, heard the noise
and was following close behind.

Grammy strategically placed the boxes in the front
yard and carefully rested the speakers on top. Buttons were
pushed, wires connected, and switches flipped, and, just
like that, La Tarántula was overcome with goose bumps,
because the very same music that had inspired her during
her childhood started blaring for everyone to hear.

"Just because you've been one way for part of your

life," said Grammy, "doesn't mean you can't change if you really want to."

Grammy didn't wait for a response. Instead, she swayed her hips and swung her arms as if she were totally lost in the music, which everyone knows is the best way to dance. Grammy's spirit was free. It was a feeling La Tarántula hadn't felt in way too long, and she knew that this was the time to either embrace the change or push it away forever.

La Tarántula walked to the speakers with purpose, and, for a moment, Grammy thought that maybe the connection to the past was too much to take. After all, you can't make someone else have fun. They have to want to make the change for themselves.

But then Grammy noticed that La Tarántula wasn't walking with anger. She wasn't mad or annoyed or fighting the music. She was turning it louder. She was seizing the moment, dancing with joy and wonder, just like a person with a strong connection to her spirit animal.

It was a connection that Grammy hadn't seen for herself in decades, not since the time she spent with Uncle Skeeta, when she recognized something in his soul that maybe he didn't even see himself, or at least not yet. There was a new light glowing in La Tarántula. Without thinking, Grammy reached into her pocket and grabbed a rock—a perfect, beautiful rock that she had carried with her for too long. Grammy knew that now was the right time to pass it on.

She held the rock tight, and things instantly froze. Grammy's body got warmer. A few seconds later, everything moved in super slow motion. There was a sharp burst of light, and then: THUMP, thump, thump, thump. THUMP, thump, thump, thump.

La Tarántula was gone. In her place was one of the most pleasant insects in the world, with bright beautiful wings that absorbed the heat from the sun and provided even more energy.

"You're a butterfly," whispered Grammy.

La Tarántula just froze, staring at Grammy as if she couldn't hear.

"Your spirit animal," Grammy repeated. "It's a butterfly."

"It's not possible," said La Tarántula, her voice quivering with emotion. "I thought I was a tarantula."

"You thought wrong," said Grammy, and the look in

her eyes made La Tarántula understand that a butterfly, in its own way, was perfect. What other animal better proves that people can change? They might start one way, like a caterpillar, and then evolve into something totally different. And deep down in her soul that felt right.

"I'm a butterfly," said La Tarántula. And that's when a great weight was lifted from her spirit, because she actually started to believe that change was possible. Grammy focused again, and instead of La Tarántula, Grammy saw Isabela with a leather cord hanging from her neck. On the leather cord was the rock, and on the rock was an imprint of wings.

"We butterflies know how to soar," said Isabela proudly. "And we love to dance."

Without another word, Isabela started moving her body to the music with rhythm and joy. Dancing is contagious, or at least it should be, and, in this case, it was. The energy from the music spread like a wave, and for reasons they couldn't even imagine, all the neighborhood kids, especially the ones from Brody's birthday adventure, showed up at Grammy's ready to boogie.

The wolverine in Halil could really move. Jared and

Brian were getting down to what looked like a combination of the cha-cha and the "just shake your body however you want." As an octopus, Ranjeta's arms had all the right motions, and Bonita proved that tiger sharks could really mosh, which is basically when everyone slams into each other, but it's to the rhythm of the music, and nobody gets hurt. Tackle do-si-doed with a couple of cool cats, and Gizmo couldn't resist the vibe and jammed on his guitar.

Even Jaylan, who once believed more in "self-preservation" than in taking on a challenge, was inspired to join what turned into the largest dance party ever on Grammy's lawn.

"What?" said Jaylan, when everyone stared in surprise that he would be interested in something so freeing and fun. "I'm not the same kid I was before. I've matured."

"It's only been a month," said Brian. "How much can you mature in a month?"

"Yeah, but it seems like three years," said Jaylan, with a wink and smirk that was well deserved.

And just like that, Jaylan started dancing with so much energy that everyone quickly forgot about his past and focused on his present, which was actually the perfect gift for Sarraka, because the circle they formed around Jaylan captured a wave of energy like a funnel of fun and channeled it through the sky directly to the magical world that needed it most.

Bumfuzzle

The sound coming from the vitality meter changed from a ringing to a dinging. The needle moved slowly from red to green as Sarraka soaked up all the energy that came from the dancing and the laughing and the fun on Grammy's front lawn. And that powerful magic made all the difference in the world.

"Grammy, you're the best," whispered Brody, staring at the needle as it continued to move in the right direction. "We have energy," Brody yelled. His voice grew louder each time he repeated those words, as he high-fived, chest-bumped, or hugged a fellow animal or friend.

Myles was quick to notice that when Brody hugged

Rosalina, she hugged him back for just the smallest of seconds longer than normal. Like any "big brother," Myles shot Brody a threatening stare. "We have the energy," Brody shrugged, as if it were a logical explanation for a prolonged hug.

Having power is one thing; knowing what to do with it is quite another. So immediately, Jake and Alec started frantically looking around, hoping for a clue about what to do next.

"Maybe this will help," smiled Punch, revealing a detailed notebook called *The Secrets of Sarraka*, which seemed to explain everything there was to know about the spirit-animal world, including how to repair the Rock of Sarraka when the pieces have been broken. After all, why would he ever give Felonious a hug unless it was to snag that very important notebook right out of his finny pack?

"El Pantsing Crab," Jake grinned. "I thought you were going to stop doing that."

"I know," said Punch with a shrug. "I'll start stopping tomorrow."

It only took a short time for Jake and Alec to review

the notebook and understand what needed to be done. Using stumps for chairs and rocks for chalk, Jake set up what looked like a classroom, which made perfect sense, because he was about to teach a lesson in how to save a magical world from certain disaster.

He carefully hung a map on the wall of the cave and grabbed a large, thin rock.

"This is Sarraka," he said, dragging the rock in a circle along the outer boundary of the map. "And it's going to implode. The question is, how do we stop it?"

Jake pointed a stick at a small cylinder-shaped object in the center of the map. "This is a cavern in the center of Sarraka," he said. "It's called The Incubator."

Rosalina looked at Brody. "You know what an incubator is, right?"

Brody shrugged and looked around. "Of course, but let's see if you know what it is."

Rosalina rolled her eyes. "It's a small, safe space that helps care and protect things that are just born, like babies."

"That's exactly right," said Jake, and Brody nodded as if to say, "That's what I was going to say, too." Although he tried to avoid a cocky grin.

"According to the research, this cavern is the original home of the Rock of Sarraka," continued Jake. "It's the place where it was formed."

Using a few charts, graphs, and diagrams, Jake explained that The Incubator contained a special kind of soil that provided the Rock of Sarraka with just the right amount of nutrients, just the right amount of oxygen. It allowed just the right amount of space for the water particles, and it was just the right temperature.

"So it's perfect," said Rosalina. "But how does that help us?"

"Remember, the Rock of Sarraka is the heart of the Pleasant Tree, and right now, it's in pieces," said Jake. "That's why Sarraka is crumbling. It's basically dying of a broken heart. But if we can restore the rock with this soil, we can restore the power to Sarraka."

"So how do we get down there?" asked Rosalina.

Jake grabbed the rock and drew two straight lines down to the cylinder. "This tunnel runs down to the same level as The Incubator. Once we jump in, we'll shoot right down. Then it's just a short walk through the core of Sarraka, and we're there."

"Define *shoot*," said Alec.

"Define *short*," said Rosalina.

"Define *bumfuzzle*," said Punch.

Jake shook his head and took a deep breath as he consulted the notebook. "*Shoot*, as in we'll be tied to a special vine called the bungee vine. It will feel like the longest, fastest, free fall you can imagine. *Short*, as in about three football fields, but this is the middle of the world, and we'll have to be prepared for anything. And as for *bumfuzzle*—it means to be confused or flustered."

"I don't get it," said Punch, looking confused and flustered.

Jake allowed a brief moment for SWEEPE to digest all the information he had explained, and then he moved on to the final piece of the mission. Once the three rocks were secured in the soil, The Incubator would immediately start to shrink to protect and harness the Rock of Sarraka. The process would only take seconds, so it was important to get out immediately.

"Just yank the bungee vine, and you'll be pulled up right away," Jake explained.

"And what if we don't get out in time?" asked Alec.

Jake said nothing, which pretty much said it all.

Was this mission even possible? they all wondered secretly.

The silence was finally broken when Rosalina stepped forward. She looked directly at Brody, Punch, and Alec. She looked for Myles, but he had gone with the rest of the animals.

"So let me get this straight," Rosalina said. "Basically, you're saying that we get the chance to do the longest bungee jump in the world, hike through the center of a magical world, and return three magical rocks to their ultimate home?" She waited just a few beats and added, "Can't think of a better way to spend an afternoon."

See Me

A confident smile formed on Brody Boondoggle's face, or it could have been the extreme speed forcing his cheeks to flap in the wind as he was shooting down the tunnel like a white-throated needletail, which is a kind of bird that can fly a hundred miles an hour, although, to be fair, that mostly happens when it's looking for a date.

Either way, when Brody finally landed in the center of Sarraka next to Jake, Alec, Punch, and Rosalina, he felt powerful and positive and ready to lead his friends on the most important journey in the world.

"I can't believe I'm stuck here with you lame ducks. The only thing strong about you guys is your breath."

Hmmmm. That was strange, thought Brody. *Did those words really come from my mouth?*

It was hard to tell from looking at Jake. He was used to that kind of talk from Brody, but the looks on the faces of Alec, Rosalina, and Punch led Brody to realize that something just a little odd must be going on.

Brody shrugged and tried to say, "I'm so sorry. I didn't mean to say that, at least not to anyone but Jake." Instead, words like *despicable, junky, stinky* and *ghastly* shot out of his mouth, and he didn't even know what *ghastly* meant (it means particularly scary, by the way).

Brody was even more confused when Rosalina looked him in the eye, offered a sweet smile, and said, "This whole mission is a disaster, which makes sense because disaster is your middle name. Or is it crotchety?" Rosalina shook her head back and forth as if she was trying to fix her brain, but it was no use.

What she didn't know was that the spirit-animal world wouldn't let just anyone play with its heart, so there were special kinds of defenses along the way, starting with an unusual kind of vapor that caused people to say things that they didn't really mean.

"One piece of advice for you clowns," Rosalina added, "don't let your minds wander because they're too small to be going off on their own."

"This is a total waste of time," said Alec, which didn't sound too unlike the normal Alec until he added, "I'd rather be in my room doing homework."

"That's enough," shouted Brody. But instead of saying something encouraging like "We have to find a way to work this out," he challenged everyone to "See me," which is a cocky way of saying "You wanna fight?" and before they knew it, Alec, Rosalina, and Brody were wrestling on the ground, while Punch shouted insults like "Is 12 your age or your IQ?" or "You don't know the meaning of the word *fear*. But, then again, you don't know the meaning of most words," or "I heard it took you an hour to make minute rice."

Wrestling against two of your friends is never easy, and it's more difficult when you have cracked ribs that feel as if you're being attacked by a bald-faced hornet, which is not quite as painful as a bullet ant but is said to feel like your hand is being crushed in a car door. Still, the wrestling match continued until Alec had the bright idea to reach for Brody's bungee vine. He got Rosalina's instead, and when he pulled, Rosalina was instantly lifted out of the cavern.

Moa Fun

Brody struggled on the ground, trying to stop a possessed Alec from grabbing his bungee vine, but that was just the start of his worries. His eyes widened when he saw Jake walk over to the scrum, roll up his sleeve, and stare down at Brody. If Jake wanted to team up with Alec, he could easily pull Brody's bungee vine, and the adventure would be over, just like that.

But instead, things instantly froze. Brody's right eye focused, and when he looked up, he could have sworn he saw a huge 12-foot-tall bird with long legs and a long neck.

You're a giant moa, Brody said to the bird, which had an unusually small brain for its size, and, sadly, was hunted until there were no moa. Brody turned his head slightly to see that there were two moa, then four moa, then eight, all running around the cave as fast as they could with no particular purpose at all.

"No, no," Brody said to the moa. "I knowa you want to help, but you're just spreading around the vapor that's causing all the trouble in the first place." Brody could feel the gas flowing faster into his lungs, which is the only reason he would say something like this: "You're just not that smart. This isn't the time for fun."

But maybe the moa deserved a little moa credit, or maybe there's never a bad time to have some fun. Either way, Brody was right. The moa the moa ran, the moa the vapor caused people to do things they didn't really mean to do—things like helping a little brother instead of hammering him.

Just as Alec was about to pull Brody's bungee vine, Jake pushed Alec away, grabbed Brody's arm, and dragged him to his feet. He brushed the dirt off Brody's shirt, smiled, and said sincerely, "It takes a lot of toughness to deal with cracked ribs. Take a second to rest, and then we'll keep going."

Brody's eyes shot open, and his jaw dropped to the ground. He wasn't alone. Rosalina, who was still connected by radio and was listening from above, and Alec, who was sitting on the ground, were speechless, which was a good thing at this point. Punch was shell-shocked, but he could still manage a few nasty thoughts. "Oh, little baby needs his big brother to help him."

Sometimes I do, thought Brody, even if he would never admit it. Then he turned to the moas. "Thank you," he said, but the moas just kept running around and around as if the only thing they were focused on was having a little moa fun.

A Quagga-mire

"You've got this, Brod. Just lead the way, and we'll be right behind you," Jake said, as the vapor continued to fill his lungs. And even though Brody knew Jake didn't really mean it, and he couldn't respond with anything nicer than, "You couldn't keep up with a garden snail," deep down Brody felt good.

He took five deep breaths, which hurt his ribs but fueled his spirit. He switched on the light on the top of his hat and took off like a gazelle, leaping over streams and ponds of hot lava before thinking of a jumping spider and running on the side of the cave walls to get around the failing bridges.

Through it all, Brody worked just as hard to control the words that came out of his mouth, but that was no use. "You guys are so slow, you couldn't beat an egg," Brody shrugged. Then he told himself that if he couldn't say anything nice, he shouldn't say anything at all.

The others did the same, with varying levels of success. "Stupid, shoddy, worthless," yelled Punch with an apologetic grin. But in the end, everyone understood that this was just the way it was going to be. People would say things they didn't mean, such as "greasy hair," "pen and pencil legs," "sewer breath" (that was Punch, too). No one would take it personally, and it wouldn't slow them down.

In that way, SWEEPE continued to overcome the defense mechanisms of Sarraka with help from the Caspian tiger, the koala lemur, and the Jamaica giant galliwasp, although not before Punch was sucked into a puddle of sludge and had to be pulled to the surface.

Brody looked down at the vitality meter to see that Sarraka had only 10 minutes of energy left. When he looked back up, he ran right into a solid, transparent wall, like a bird flying into a glass window. The Clarity Barrage was the last line of protection before The Incubator.

"This isn't good," said Alec.

"Everything makes sense in Sarraka," pleaded Rosalina. "There has to be a way."

Time continued to tick as Jake searched for a handle or some kind of opener, and Alec pounded on the wall with a log. Even Rosalina and Punch, still connected by radio, offered several suggestions, but the wall would not move. "Let's go, Brodeo," said Jake in a calm, controlled voice. "You see things other people don't. Use those powers of yours. What do you see now?"

"Oh, brother," said Alec. "Who are you and what have you done with the real Jake? I think I'm going to throw up."

It's amazing what a little support can do, and right then was a perfect example of how *nice* is stronger than *mean*. Brody actually listened to Jake, trying to see things that other people didn't, and that's when his pink eye helped him see a creature with stripes in the front like a zebra and soft, brown hair in the back like a horse.

"A quagga," whispered Brody, and the unusual-looking creature that unfortunately had become extinct because it was easy to find and hunt, responded with its standard cry of "kwa-ha-ha," which is how it got its name.

"But how can you help?" Brody whispered, as the badger in Alec continued to alternate between punching, kicking, and head-butting the solid barrier as hard as he could.

The quagga said nothing, because as we know, that's not how it works. Time was running out, and the vapor-infected part of Brody was losing his patience. Why would an animal that was half one thing and half another come to help? Why couldn't it be a parrot, or even an ant, which was pretty good at communicating with its buddies?

Then Brody looked at the stripes on the zebra side of the quagga. Most were straight lines, but there was one that was different—kind of like a white arrow—and Brody suddenly understood that no other animal could be a better fit.

Eight minutes left.

chapter
56

Teacher's Pet

Using the arrow as his guide, Brody rushed to the other side of the cave, dropped to his knees, and started dusting away the dirt and debris.

It's got to be here somewhere, Brody thought, and before he could explain how he knew to look for something that was part one thing and part another, Brody uncovered a computerized keypad. It was just below an inscription etched into the stone.

"Thank you," Brody whispered to the quagga, who called back "kwa-ha-ha," which probably meant it was going back to graze peacefully in the meadows of Sarraka, hopefully for a very long time.

Brody immediately turned back to the inscription and read it aloud: "I'm the only number you get when you follow the alphabet."

"What the devil is that supposed to mean?" typed Alec in the keypad.

"That is an incorrect answer," said an electronic voice.

"What do you mean, incorrect?" typed Alec, still affected by the vapor. "You want to dance? Let's dance." He picked up a rock and started hitting the device.

"That, too, is an incorrect response," the electronic voice repeated. "You are down to your final guess."

"Final guess? I'll take as many guesses as I want," Alec typed and he was about to press ENTER when Jake pushed him away.

"Let's go, guys, this is something that will be fun to do together," said Jake. "Let's start brainstorming."

"I'm the only number you get when you follow the alphabet," repeated Brody again and again, walking around in circles.

"Maybe it's as simple as placing the numbers in order, just like the alphabet," suggested Jake. He grabbed a stick and in the dirt he wrote 1, 2, 3, 4. But that seemed too easy.

"The last letter of the alphabet is *Z*," said Brody. "Maybe it's the number that starts with *Z*: zero." Brody wrote *zero* in the sand. That seemed too random.

"Why couldn't that zebra-horse thing just give us the answer?" snapped Alec. "I mean what are we supposed to do, just spell out all the numbers in the sand?"

He grabbed the stick and started writing: *One, two, three, four.* A moment later, Rosalina yelled in the radio, "That's it. I think I got it."

Brody sprinted to the keyboard and typed in the five letters Rosalina listed: "*F-O-R-T-Y.*" There was a soft ding, ding, ding. As the door started to slowly open from the bottom, Rosalina explained that *forty* was the only number that was spelled with letters in alphabetical order.

"Teacher's pet," Brody muttered. He was trying to stop himself from saying something worse when he noticed that the door that had been slowly rising was now going back down, and it wasn't going slowly.

Without hesitation, Jake bolted like an ocelot and dove under the falling door. Alec was about to dive to the other side when he saw Brody. He wasn't going to make it. The door was falling too fast.

The power of the vapor urged Alec to keep going and think only of himself, but his spirit animal was fighting back as hard as it could—and there are few things stronger than the will of a badger. So instead of diving through the opening, Alec cupped his hands on the bottom of the door and lifted with all his might.

"Go," he grimaced.

The door slowed down just barely, but it was just barely enough for Brody to slide underneath. When he did, Alec's grip weakened, and the door came crashing down. Alec immediately tried typing in the code again, but the electronic voice simply said, "Nice try, big guy, but that's not happening."

"You're not happening," barked Alec, who could only sit and cheer on his friends. "I have no faith in you," he yelled, yanking on the bungee vine, and when he did, he shot up into the sky like a firecracker. "I'll be waiting here when you fail."

Six minutes.

Shhlurp

The Incubator was a relatively small room with rounded walls, like a hut or a rounded tent known as a *yurt*. Brody scooped up a small sample of the dark, rich soil that covered almost every inch of the ground. It felt soft and soothing, and as he continued to move it around his fingers, a peaceful calm swept over his entire body.

This is where we belong, Brody thought. He could feel it in his soul, which inspired his spirit and carried him to the other side of the hut. There he found a wall that was completely covered in gray mud, except for three distinct holes that were the exact shape and size of the three parts of the Rock of Sarraka.

Brody looked at Jake, who looked back as if to say, "This is why we're here, right?" Careful not to say anything that would ruin the moment, Brody simply nodded and reached into the bag with the pieces of the first rock that Rudy had broken.

Five minutes.

It was just like doing a puzzle. Brody and Jake worked together as Brody rotated and rearranged the pieces in just the right ways until they fit perfectly together in the middle hole. A small bead of sweat formed on Brody's brow as he slowly pushed the rock deeper into the slot, until he heard a soft suction sound. Shhlurp.

Four minutes.

"One down, Brodacious," said Jake. "You can do this. We can do it together."

The vapor was still working on Brody, so he was having a tougher time ignoring the fact that Jake didn't really mean a word he said. And even so, they were just words. "Might as well enjoy it while you can," commented Rosalina. "Yeah," added Alec. "Because most of us are pretty sure you are going to find a way to mess this up."

Jake smiled. Brody smiled, and then he reached for

the second bag with all the broken pieces that made up the second part of the rock. He and Jake repeated the puzzle process that had worked before. Shhlurp.

Three minutes.

Brody took a deep, satisfying breath and wiped the sweat from his forehead. It was almost over, or maybe it was just the beginning. Even if he saved Sarraka, things could get much worse. It had taken all his will, all his power just to find Punching Crab, get back to Sarraka, and defeat Felonious. What would it take to defeat a force that was probably even stronger?

Brody quickly cleared his mind of such thoughts. This last rock would be the easiest—it was still in one piece— and all Brody and Jake had to do was insert the rock into the final hole, pull their bungee vines, and Sarraka would be saved. A puppy could do it.

Brody removed the final piece from his bag, repeated the ritual a third time, and waited for that sweet suction sound that meant everything would be beautiful again, if only for a short time. The problem was, there was no sound. When Brody placed the rock into the last hole, it fit, but it did not stay connected. Brody's and Jake's eyes moved in unison, following the rock as it slid down the wall, slowly and steadily, until it hit the ground.

"How could this be?" Rosalina blurted. "Did Rudy break that rock when we weren't looking?" Jake turned to Brody, who seemed frozen with a blank, frightened look on his face. He knew the truth.

"Rudy didn't make this happen," said Brody. "The nothingness did."

One Solution

Brody Boondoggle frantically picked up the final piece of the rock and placed it back in the hole. He got the same result. He did it again and again, jamming the rock into the hole in the wall, but forcing things rarely makes them work, or at least not as they're supposed to, and it didn't work that time either.

Two minutes.

"Why would the nothingness do that?" asked Rosalina. "I thought it wanted to take Sarraka alive, slowly drain all its resources. If something doesn't hold that rock in place, Sarraka will be destroyed, and the nothingness will lose."

An ice cold chill swept through the cave as the two

brothers just stared at each other, neither wanting to say a word, even though they both realized what the someone or something behind this nothingness had done. It would actually seem quite clever if it weren't so cruel.

It was clear that Brody was going to save Sarraka. And it was also clear that he would lead the charge against whatever danger would come next. So this nothingness changed the game. If Brody wanted to save Sarraka, he would have to sacrifice himself. He would have to hold the final piece of the rock on the wall and let The Incubator crumble around him. He wouldn't be around to fight. Or, he could pull his bungee cord, fly to the surface, and get out before Sarraka crumbled to the ground.

Brody had to make a choice.

Sixty seconds.

"I'll do it," said Brody, breaking the uncomfortable silence. "I'm going to stay here and hold the rock. After all, this is the Brodeo."

Brody took a deep breath. Now that he said those words, made the decision, he felt good, especially when he looked in the eyes of his big brother. Brody immediately recognized the expression, even if he had only seen it in his dreams. It was respect, which just might be the greatest gift a big brother can give. Then the expression changed to one of worry and concern, which would make sense if it weren't coming from Jake.

"This is a good decision," said Brody reassuringly, meaning he was trying to convince Jake of what he already knew. "The universe needs Sarraka," Brody said. He paused for a second. "I'm sorry about those things I said before. I didn't mean them."

Thirty seconds.

"Yes, you did," said Jake, and Brody shrugged.

Of course, Jake knew Brody was right. This was his fight, and a feeling of pride consumed Jake's heart, because he could see the sincerity in Brody's eyes. Instead of being a cocky little brother, Brody was willing to risk everything for something he cared about more than himself, because that's what real heroes do. This was, after all, the only choice he could make. But that didn't mean it was the only choice.

Jake was thinking of something he could say to Brody, something that would show how he really felt, but words can seem so unimportant. Actions speak so much louder. So Jake moved closer to his little brother. "This nothingness is obviously scared of you. Don't forget that." Then he gave his little brother a hug and whispered, "The universe needs Brody Boondoggle, too. Toughen up."

And before Brody could understand that maybe Jake had control of his words all along, Jake pushed Brody to the opening of The Incubator and pulled the bungee vine on his back. In an instant, Brody was pulled farther and farther away from his big brother, just when he felt they were closest.

Jake waited for Brody to be out of sight and safe. Then he pointed two fingers to his eyes and two in the direction of the rock. "You're staying down, once and for all."

Fifteen seconds.

Jake didn't rush. He simply picked up the final rock, and that's when he felt something strange but weirdly familiar, as if a distant memory had been unlocked. Jake dropped to his knees, and in that moment, he finally realized what Grammy meant about the power of connections.

Ten seconds.

Jake focused on that power and willed himself to his feet. Then, with his last burst of spirit, Jake lunged for the wall and held the rock in just the right space until he heard that subtle sucking sound that meant the Rock of Sarraka was home where it belonged.

5, 4, 3, 2... Shhlurp.

chapter
59

Not Alone

Brody Boondoggle stayed in Sarraka for one more perfect sunset that he shared with Alec, Punch, and, especially, Rosalina. Sitting under the Pleasant Tree, which was healthy and strong, they talked very little, except to say things like, "I can't believe Jake did what he did," or "Where do you think he is now?" or "Would you rather have a dragon or be a dragon?"

As the sun finally dipped over the horizon, and night took its turn for the day, Brody searched his spirit for that same peaceful calm that meant everything would somehow be okay. He took five deep breaths and closed his eyes, hoping his special connection to the auras of the land would help him see visions of what the future might hold.

He could sense that Jake wasn't hurt, at least not seriously. Maybe it was good that Jake never believed. After all, if you don't truly believe in magic, then you can't be truly affected by it. But Brody also remembered what could happen to any kid who tried to touch the Rock of Sarraka without just the right amount of power—he could lose his spirit animal or worse.

And even though Sarraka was safe, it was only for now. Brody could feel the danger that was coming, and he had no idea how to stop it.

It was just a short hike back to the Aka Lair, where the Akaway was starting to feel better in all the right ways. Brody brought a basket filled with apples and avocados and placed it next to the cave.

"It seems every time I try to make things better, they somehow get worse," Brody said softly. "I hope I made the right choice."

Brody's right eye started to tingle. It wasn't painful, just persistent, and when Brody closed his eyes, he heard a wise voice from deep inside his soul.

"You made the only choice," said the Akaway. "Just look at what you have done. You made more of a difference than you ever realized, and, for that, we will always be grateful."

Brody followed his instincts and turned his head to look into the distance. He allowed himself a soft smile as he saw all the spirit animals and extinct animals of Sarraka jumping and running and playing, just like they were meant to do. He felt even better when he saw Rosalina hugging an extinct swift fox who finally seemed at home.

Brody nodded to Myles, who stared back as if to stay, "Be good to my sister, because I'll be watching." He also left Brody a gift. Now Brody would have a Hoodster of his own.

Brody turned to Punching Crab. "Are you sure you won't come back with us?" But Brody already knew the answer. Punching Crab was staying in Sarraka. He would work with Myles, the Akaway, and the rest of the animals to start preparing for whatever was coming next, even though the thought of the nothingness made his shell boil with fear. "Laga, laga, laga."

And then, with a simple golden acorn, Brody, Rosalina,

and Alec were gone, magically transported back to their homes through the perfect wall of smoke. Alec fell fast asleep, while Brody and Rosalina lay awake in their beds until they finally decided to give up on sleep and get right to their dreams.

Rosalina climbed out of her window and sat on a brand-new chair made just for her balcony. Moments later, Isabela joined her granddaughter, and for the first time in a long time, they talked, and more importantly, listened and stared at the perfect view of an endless sea of stars.

Isabela looked at her beautiful granddaughter. The timid, tired girl who seemed to have given up so long ago was gone. In her place was a vibrant spirit that beamed with self-confidence and strength. "I'm so proud of you," she said with a smile, and Rosalina smiled back because at that moment, she truly believed anything was possible.

As for Brody, his mind was someplace else, maybe even connected to his brother. He placed his Hoodster safely in the closet, and then slowly walked from his room to Jake's, hoping that maybe he was there. Instead, he found Tackle lying at the foot of the bed and Grammy sitting next to him, wearing her buffalo flannel pajamas and long, blue housecoat. She was rubbing that special place behind Tackle's ears and explaining in perfect dog Spanish that there was no need to worry about Jake, because two brothers working together just might be the greatest magic in the universe.

"You really think so?" asked Brody. "You think everything that happened, happened for a reason?"

"I guess we'll find out," said Grammy softly. "But I do know this. The Rock of Sarraka is safe and protected, and now spirit animals will always have a place to live and laugh and explore. And I couldn't imagine a world without spirit animals. Could you?"

The Man With the Silver Hair

That night, a dark car with tinted windows was clearly in spy mode as it carefully followed a person who seemed like just an ordinary guy, even if everyone knows there's no such thing.

The man was average height with a full head of thick, silver hair. He was out for a midnight stroll on a beautiful night, but didn't appear particularly happy or sad or anything at all, even though everything was finally exactly the way he wanted it.

"What are we doing here?" asked Rudy, rolling down the window just a crack so he could get a better look. "Who is that man?"

Felonious didn't answer. Instead, he turned to Uncle Skeeta, who handed Rudy a special pair of sunglasses that he had created just for this occasion. Rudy gasped when he put on the glasses, because this normal-looking man looked like something very different.

"That's exactly what you see," said Felonious, as he slowly rolled up the window. "That is nothingness."

Ready to find
YOUR
Spirit Animal?

Visit brodyboondoggle.com
and follow Gary on Twitter (@garykarton),
Instagram (@garykarton)
and Facebook.com/Gary Karton.

————— **Coming Soon:** —————
Book Three in the
Brody Boondoggle series

About the Author

In third grade, a teacher explained to Gary that he had a learning disability. "You learn things differently from most kids," she said. "But different is good."

Still, Gary spent his life struggling to read. Surprisingly, he grew up to become a writer, first as a reporter for *The Washington Post* and then as a speechwriter and author.

When Gary had kids of his own, he wanted to inspire them to enjoy stories and books and creativity and imagination. So, he read to them—*Dr. Seuss, A Series of Unfortunate Events, Peter and the Star Catchers*, and many more.

At one point, Gary's kids predicted the ending to a book they were reading and challenged Gary to write a book for kids with an ending you'd never see coming. He accepted the challenge, and the Brody Boondoggle series was born.

Author's Note

As a kid, I was sometimes criticized for daydreaming. My mind would just wander off, and all of a sudden I'd be lost in my imagination. It's still one of my favorite places to be (I also love the dog park). Either way, this book would not have been possible without all the people in my life who were willing to dream along with me.

That starts with the kids who read early drafts to make sure I was on the right track. Brielle (and her mom, Lauren), Ryan, Maggie, Owen, and Sophie. Thanks a ton to Ian and Graeme, and their mom, Kelly, who still appreciates the halibut joke.

Troy for reminding me about the power of clouds, and Jared for always being willing to brainstorm. Thanks to Hunter, too, for being beautifully original.

Will and Ella are examples of everything that is good about kids. Thanks to the Braggs (Brady, Kai, Colby, Canon, Mark, and Jacki), for sharing their creativity so freely (what a great gift); and the McGinley-Smiths (Sage, Mica, Ezra, Dan, and Sarah), who always seem to be in the middle of a great adventure.

Thanks to John Karzen, one of the most generous

people I know. It takes a special kind of friendship to give away a book instead of a jersey as a prize for a basketball camp, but that's what he did again and again. John truly understands the importance of fun, and I've been lucky to be along for the ride since I was 10.

Thanks to Dave, who is willing to drive as long as it takes to come up with nothingness. Thanks to Susan for being honest, Rachel for being awesome, and Poppy for sharing these books with every kid he knows.

Thanks to Shannon and Erin, and to Torine, Martha, and everyone at Safe Kids—you are true heroes. Sam for your talent, and Rich and everyone at Brattle for believing in this story.

Moms don't always get the thanks they deserve, and sometimes brothers and sisters don't either. This project would not have been possible without my mom's support in so many ways. But most of all, she's there for us, and I wanted to say thanks for everyone to hear. That goes for Devora and Jeff, too.

Finally, thanks to Dixie, Jake, and Brody (and Halea, too). I could mention that Brody read every draft, Dixie sacrificed her Mother's Day, Halea is an everyday inspiration, and I know Jake wouldn't want me to list the many ways he contributed. But beyond the obvious, they remind me every day that true connections really matter, that there is nothing more powerful than love, and that there's real magic in dreaming.